The
Seekers of Shar-Nuhn

ARDATH MAYHAR

DOUBLEDAY & COMPANY, INC.

GARDEN CITY, NEW YORK

1980

All of the characters in this book
are fictitious, and any resemblance
to actual persons, living or dead,
is purely coincidental.

First Edition

ISBN 0-385-15623-5
Library of Congress Catalog Card Number 79–7887
Copyright © 1980 by Ardath Mayhar
All Rights Reserved
Printed in the United States of America

I

Three Secrets

This is Shar-Nuhn on the Purple Waters. Strong are the walls of Shar-Nuhn and deep her treasuries, for her fleets ply all the seas and gather riches for the canny Shar-Neen.

This is a city of secrets—small secrets, whispered in shadows; great secrets, hidden in temples. Secrets of wealth, secrets of crimes, secrets of conspirators, but in the city of Shar-Nuhn there are three secrets of paramount importance. The first of the Three Great Secrets teaches the seafarers of Shar-Nuhn to quiet the waters, in time of storm; wherefore no laden ship, no humble sailor of Shar-Nuhn is ever lost at sea.

The Second Secret is terrible truly, for it enables the Shar-Neen to trouble the lands to their foundations, as their enemies learned to their cost, in ages agone. Covetous eyes long envied Shar-Nuhn her riches, and an army marched forth for conquest. When the earth quaked and cracked before them, and their cities crumbled to rubble behind them, they turned up their eyes in despair and removed their place of abode, and sought no longer to trouble Shar-Nuhn.

But the Third Secret is a secret indeed, and none knows of it save the oldest of the Initiates in the Temple

of Truth. Rumor says that it is the secret of illimitable
wealth, or that it gives unending life and vigor, but there
is only one who knows, and his life is dedicated to the
preservation of the Third Secret of Shar-Nuhn.

Now there are those to whom the existence of a secret
is a challenge—even a pain. It is an itch unscratched, a
hunger unsatisfied. Such was the nature of Kla-Noh, the
Seeker. Secrets had been his livelihood, for he purveyed
his wares among the members of the Guild of Thieves,
among the great merchants, among the wives and hus-
bands of the rich. No secret was too poor and threadbare
to arouse his interest. All were small itches, and he
scratched them profitably. Naturally, the greater and
more valuable the secret, the greater was the itch of Kla-
Noh. And the Third Secret of Shar-Nuhn was the agony
and the terrible unscratched itch of his life.

Though he knew well many of the Initiates, never
would he ask of them. It would be worth much, in terms
of wealth, to the Seeker who dared seek it in the Temple
of Truth, but that was not the thing that tortured Kla-
Noh. The thought of the secret itself tantalized him. To
be the co-possessor of the Third Secret of Shar-Nuhn,
having wrested it, unaided, from the Tower—surely there
could be no higher aspiration for a Seeker After Secrets.
To be able to fondle it in the private recesses of his mind,
knowing that only one other on the planet could do the
same, would be the finest sort of wealth for one like Kla-
Noh. It would be a fitting climax and finale to his career,
setting his seal upon his craft, as its one and unapproach-
able master. Then, and only then, could he retire to his
modest villa and vineyard and spend his declining years
sitting in the sun, considering the meanings of existence,
probing into the questions that fill the universe, while the
Purple Waters lapped the shore below his terrace.

On an evening in the dark of the moon, Kla-Noh descended his terrace to his small landing, got into his light sailing craft, and wafted gently across the curve of the bay to the harbor, where the great wharves lifted black bulks against the stars. Leaving his tethered craft dancing lightly upon the lipping wavelets, he made his way to a drinking place, where gathered the sailors and the harbor people. Kla-Noh sought a helper, for the Tower that was the Temple of Truth had been raised, by remarkable arts, from the floor of the sea and stood alone outside the protecting arm of the bay. One needed the aid of a man skilled in the arts of the sea, for the Purple Waters flung themselves strongly about the Tower of Truth, and any save the skilled found themselves swamped and sunk and drawn away into the mysteries of the sea.

There was a fair company at the Sign of the Dolphins, and Kla-Noh found a place in a shadowed corner and set himself to examine his companions. Most were bluff, wind-burned seamen with pale eyes, which seemed always to be looking into deep skies and boundless oceans. There were a handful of shopkeepers and clerks from the warehouses. At the long table beneath the window sat a grim-faced and red-haired young man, who wrapped his hands about his glass and gazed into it as if seeking the ends of all being therein. He was huddled in a ragged cloak, and his shoes were mere collections of holes. This man interested Kla-Noh, if for no other reason than that he had the look of one with secrets of his own, and any secret at all drew Kla-Noh like a magnet.

The Seeker bought a bottle of fair wine, then made his way to the long table and sat beside the man in the ragged cloak. After a lengthy moment, the ragged man's green eyes reluctantly left his glass and sought his unexpected companion. Something in the face of the Seeker seemed to amuse him, for he chuckled low in his chest.

"May I share your joke, my friend?" asked Kla-Noh. "And I shall gladly share with you my wine."

"Sit. Sit and be welcome, old man. You have the look of a Seeker. I, Si-Lun, have sought somewhat myself, and have a feeling for the craft." He moved down the stained bench, making room, and Kla-Noh poured generously from his bottle.

"You seem a stranger here," said Kla-Noh. "Shar-Nuhn can be more lonely than a star to a stranger without friends or family."

"All places are lonely to me, Seeker," answered the ragged man. "All lonely, alike, and all empty. The sea is my family and friend, my road and home."

The heart of Kla-Noh was touched, for he was a kindly man. And he thought, too, that one so ragged and rootless would be eager to help in his enterprise. His shrewd and withered features wrinkled in a smile, and he said to the ragged man, "If it will please you, I shall provide you with that which may substitute for family and friend, which will provide the home and make easier the road. And in return . . ."

"And in return . . ." echoed the man, and his eyes glowed greenly with strange laughter, and his lips twisted bitterly.

"I ask only your skill as a sailor, that is all. For one little hour—perhaps two. And if your old calling as a Seeker should urge you to aid me more, then I should welcome and reward such help."

Si-Lun looked deeply into his eyes, lifted his glass, and said, "I shall give you aid. Tell me your plan, that I may know what it is that I promise."

And Kla-Noh took him across the curve of the bay, to the landing where the waters lipped and lapped against the shore at the foot of his terrace. Deep into the night they sat beneath the wheeling stars, speaking softly in darkness, and now and again they would look far out, beyond the arm of the bay, where the Tower of Truth was only a speck of white light against the sea and the sky.

* * *

In a month, when again the moon rode below the horizon, they had completed their plan. A strongly ribbed dory bore them out of the bay and into the full surge of the Purple Waters. Si-Lun strove mightily with the oars, rowing them swiftly toward the Tower, as Kla-Noh sat, silent, thinking of the secret he longed to know.

Where the waters rolled and tumbled about the foot of the Tower, Si-Lun's skill was sorely tried, but he was adept, and he brought the dory to rest at last at the foot of the steps that led from the floor of the sea to the door of the Temple of Truth. There were those who said that, at times, the Initiates had been seen to descend those stairs and to disappear beneath the waters, as those who, descending a mountain, pass through a layer of cloud. None could say truly, for the ways of the Initiates are not the ways of mortal men.

But Si-Lun and Kla-Noh were not concerned with any tales save that of the Third Secret of Shar-Nuhn. They carefully tethered their dory, then made their silent way up the great stair to the door of the Temple. The door, as the law said it must, swung open to a touch, and Kla-Noh peered cautiously within. No voice, no footstep was to be heard. The spiraling stair rose into the silent Tower, and all the doors were closed upon the inner chambers. Yet the hall and the stair were brightly lit, for the law said that Truth must never stand in darkness.

So the two Seekers entered into the Tower and set

their feet upon the stairway. And at the first doorway they stopped to read the writing upon the door. It said: "THIS IS THE CHAMBER OF THE FIRST SECRET, A QUIET SPELL, FOR THE USE OF SEAFARERS. ENTER, AND WELCOME." But they passed on.

Round and round they went, past the doors of the Initiates' chambers, and came to THE CHAMBER OF THE SECOND SECRET, A DANGEROUS DEVICE. SEEK COUNSEL BEFORE ENTERING. And they passed on.

Up they went, past rank after rank of closed doors, and came at last to a door across the stair, whereon was written: "CLIMB NO HIGHER IN THE TOWER OF TRUTH, FOR THAT WHICH LIES BEYOND CONCERNS NO MORTAL MAN." The door yielded to the touch.

Behind it stood a man.

The two Seekers looked upon him with awe and with dread, for his was a face scarred by long suffering, ravaged by unthinkable years. His eyes seemed to have looked upon nothing save agony and death, pain and torment.

He stretched out his hands before him and said, "The Creator of Truth has sent you at last to relieve me of my burden. It is written that, when the toll of the years grows too great upon the Oldest Initiate, there will be sent a substitute. The secret that you seek lies in the inner chamber. Go, either or both, and examine it. Yet I am required to tell you one thing. He who lifts the burden of the secret must bear it, as I have done, that I may go free. Each day I have gazed upon the workings of the secret. Each night I have meditated upon its purposes. Look upon my face: there you will see its reflection. Only death may erase its mark from me." He folded his hands in the sleeves of his robe and stood silent, under their gaze.

Long they looked upon him. Then Kla-Noh turned to Si-Lun, and each looked into the eyes of the other. With one accord, they went down through the Temple of Truth, got into their dory, and rowed away. Some itches, Kla-Noh realized, are better left unscratched.

II

The Cat with the Sapphire Eyes

Kla-Noh sat upon his terrace, looking over the silken furrows that ridged the Purple Waters. His heart was leaden beneath his green robe, and his hands fidgeted in his lap. He said nothing, but now and again he breathed a deep sigh, gazing across the curve of the bay toward the Tower of Truth.

Then his companion would nod in sympathy and offer him fruit or wine. For Si-Lun knew what it was that troubled the old Seeker After Secrets, and his heart also was full of unrest.

"We must not look back, my friend," he said at last to Kla-Noh. "The world is full of secrets. To let our hearts yearn over one, no matter how great, is not the course of wise men. We looked into each other's eyes and turned our backs on the great secret of Shar-Nuhn, and now we must busy our hands with other things."

The old Seeker turned his eyes upon Si-Lun, as one waking from a dream. "Other things?" he asked. "But I have retired from my profession. No longer do I sniff in the shadows for secrets to peddle in the hidden places. I have no need for more riches than I possess. And small, tawdry secrets no longer tease my palate. The great secret was strong wine, though we only sniffed at it. It has spoiled my taste for the petty and the trivial."

As he spoke, his servant approached from the house door. Now he folded his hands and bowed his head and said, "My master, there is one who would speak with you."

Kla-Noh raised his grizzled brows. "Now who would be seeking an old man dreaming by the bayside?"

"One of the Great Ones, it seems to me, Lord," answered the servant. "Her robes are fine, though simple, and her bearing noble."

"Then I will go in to her," said the Seeker, and he rose and sought the arm of his friend.

Within the high-ceilinged receiving room waited one who filled it with her aura. The two Seekers looked into her eyes, then bowed low.

The lady rose from her chair and looked upon them with eyes the color of smoke across summer-blue sky. She extended her fan and directed them to rise, and with a dip and a swirl of her wrist indicated chairs, and they all sat.

"Lady," said Kla-Noh, "you honor my house. What service may this old and useless Seeker perform in your behalf?"

She glanced slantwise at Si-Lun and spoke softly. "It is a secret matter, Wise One. Is this a confidant?"

The old man smiled. "This is Si-Lun, my strong young hands and sturdy legs in my elder days. He is a Seeker himself, and other things, many of them secrets in themselves."

Her pointed chin dipped into the cup of her lotus hand as she studied the two.

"Some tale I have heard whispered," she said, "of two who mounted through the Tower of Truth to the very top, but were wise enough to turn their backs upon the Third Secret of Shar-Nuhn. Such wisdom, coupled with an affinity for . . . secrets . . . and the ability to ferret out that which is hidden, for these I have need. I have lost the Cat with the Sapphire Eyes, and it must be found before my father returns from his voyaging. You perhaps know my father," she said to Kla-Noh. "He is the merchant lord Tro-Ven."

The old man's face seemed to shrink upon its bones. His breath hissed through his teeth as he answered, "Some little dealing have I had with that noble and . . . talented . . . lord. But that he had a daughter I had never heard, and secrets are—were—my stock in trade."

"Your tact, old one, is gentle, for you do not mention that my father is also a powerful warlock. He it was who found the First Secret of Shar-Nuhn, for he had need to still the savage waters for the protection of his fleet. Something he had to do with the Second Secret, and his enemies have known the earth to tremble beneath them. And I am his daughter, whom he has sought to conceal from the eyes of men and even the ears of rumor. Little does he love me, but so long as I have my talisman . . . which I have lost. Lost! Oh, help me, Seeker, for I am in dire need!"

"Gladly would I, Lady, but I have never been a finder of lost objects," the old man whispered.

"But this object is a terrible secret also," she cried. "It is a powerful thing, and its loss must be even more a secret than its existence. And if you can find it, I may be able to enrich you beyond your dreams."

"Not riches do I need," said the Seeker quietly. "But I will help you in your need, for I am old and need useful work to do until I find my grave."

The lady bowed her head into her hands for one

heartbeat, then lifted her chin and said to the two, "You have my gratitude, do you succeed or fail, for there are few in these days who will succor the needful for that poor coin. And I am, or shall be again, powerful when my talisman is in its place."

She stood abruptly, and her gray robe moved lightly about her. "I can be away from my place for only a short time. The simulacrum that I left cannot endure for long to deceive my watchers. And it is dangerous for me to attempt the deception more than once. Know you my' father's house?" she asked Kla-Noh, who nodded.

"Upon the seaward side there is a buttressed seawall, rooted in the deeps. The years have riven it and the creatures have worn it away into paths for their own uses. One who came from the sea"—and here she looked at them from the depths of purpose—"would find no guard and no watcher, for my father fears nothing from that direction. Each evening I walk there, to watch the darkness rise from the east. Then I am unwatched, for none can approach save through my father's house."

Kla-Noh coughed. "There are ways of watching that the watched cannot know."

She smiled grimly. "When the watched are but normal men . . . or women, it is so. But I am the daughter of my father, and also the daughter of my mother. And my mother, O Seeker, is a secret that even you may find it difficult to winnow from the past. Oh, be sure, I know when I am overseen."

"Then, by your leave, there will be intruders upon the paths of the creatures," said the old man, "three evenings hence, lest by chance this day's deception might have roused suspicions. Walk round about the edges of the terrace, and we will lie close under the edge, wherever is best concealed and easiest of access for my old limbs."

The lady nodded slowly. "Often I speak with the empty sea and the sky," she mused, "and should any see, they would not wonder at it."

She took her leave, and the two Seekers stood beneath the arbor at the door and watched as she drifted away across the meadow as a wisp of smoke moves on the wind. Before she had gone many paces she was a shadow, and then she was not to be seen.

Kla-Noh lifted his brows. "That is a strange lady, my young friend," he said. "There are secrets beyond secrets there. For I have heard before of the mysteries of the Lord Tro-Ven, and once I heard a breath of a rumor . . . the merest wisp of conjecture . . . concerning a powerful talisman that he brought from afar. Only that fact, and a name. The Cat with the Sapphire Eyes. . . ."

* * *

The ghost of a new moon hung dimly in the west on the evening of the tryst. Si-Lun made Kla-Noh comfortable amidships and, under a reefed sail, scudded quietly across the bay, cutting in toward shore beneath the curve of overhanging cliff long before he reached the house of Tro-Ven. The buttressed seawall bulked darkly in the waning light as the craft hove to in its shadow.

A way to the top was soon found, for, as the lady had said, the wall was greatly worn away and was nearly as easy to climb as a flight of steps, though the footing was uncertain. Near the top they found a spot in the lee of a thorny bush that had thrust its toes into the crevices and flung masses of golden bloom down the slope. The lip of the terrace was just above, and they waited in silence for the lady to come.

The Purple Waters grew darker as the light withdrew, but before darkness descended they heard the light tap of heels on stone and knew that their companion had come.

"Who now will answer me from the sea and the sky this night?" came her musing whisper. "Many nights have I cried to the wind without succor, but mayhap this time it will be different."

"Aye, Lady, it will," said Si-Lun softly. "We are here, beneath the golden flowers."

"How fitting." She laughed. "No man ever brought me flowers, but now flowers bring me two men to champion my cause."

Kla-Noh sneezed irritably and said, "All very well, but they tickle my nose and drip pollen in my beard. Let us say what is to be said and have done."

Instantly the lady was contrite. "My apologies, Seeker," she said. "It ill befits one of your age and wisdom to crouch on a seawall in the night mist to listen to banter. I will begin by telling you my name, which is a secret to all but my father, my mother, and me. This to prove my trust, as well as to aid your endeavor. My mother (of whom I will tell you more) called me Li-Ah, and though my father willed that I be called otherwise, that is my name. In the tongue of my mother's folk, it means Fruit of Truthfulness, and for this reason it angered my father past endurance. For if you know aught of him you know that truth is not his friend or his companion.

"You must know also that my mother is not of this place. Yet the way to her realm lies not across the Purple Waters, nor yet over the barren lands to the west. My father found it when he was about his journeyings, those voyages which he makes, not in a vessel of this world, but in a powered crystal that bears him through the edges of here and into otherwhere. He found her realm, he saw her, and he desired her, for her beauty is marvelous and her wisdom wonderful.

"Yet not in all things is she wise, for, seeing Tro-Ven and finding him different from all that she knew, she chose to wed him, knowing him not as he was but as he wished to appear. And when he had learned what he could of the arts of her country and taken what he could of the riches of her father, and tired of her love, he chose to depart as he came, leaving her with an empty heart—until I came.

"There was I born and there nurtured until I became a woman grown. My mother was my friend and my teacher, my guide and my benefactress, and she taught me all that she knew. Yet always she feared that one day my father might return and claim me as his child, to bear me away into this other world, so different from her own. So she tutored me in mysteries that only those of her own blood may know or practice, hoping that they would be useful to me, wherever I should be. And she placed within a talisman a part of herself to act as a focus for my powers and my arts, at need. And that talisman is the Cat with the Sapphire Eyes. Without it I can do much, but not, I fear, so much as my father. With it I can best him and thwart his purposes, when they mean me harm."

Kla-Noh had listened in silence, but without surprise. "Somewhat of this I expected to hear," he said. "But if your father came for you and brought you as his daughter to his home, why should he seek your harm?"

"Well asked, had he brought me as his daughter," she said. "But he did not. He brought me as his talisman, even as the Cat is mine. He found that many of the arts learned in my mother's realm were ineffective save when practiced by those of her blood. So he returned, hoping, expecting that a child of his had been born to her, and took me away, over her agony and my tears. But the law is the law, there as here, and a father disposes of his child as he will. So long," she whispered grimly, "as the child will let him."

"Ah," sighed Kla-Noh. "And I'll warrant that you are not his daughter to his servants, eh? And none outside the house has heard of your existence. So he intends to use you in his secret practices. But, my dear lady, it is inevitably true that a man obsessed is half blind, and it seems to me that he has never looked at you as the powerful person you are. Is it not true that he sees you only as he wishes you to be, an instrument of his will, brought into being by himself for his own purposes?"

"True, Seeker. You are a man learned in the ways of men. Thus it is and has been, and I have said little and done nothing to rouse in him the notion that I may have a will of my own. In small things I have aided him, yet I have watched the way they are trending, and I fear in my soul's soul that he means harm to my mother and to her people. For her father is now dead, and she rules in that place beyond the wall of time. My father is no king, and his jealousy is bitter. He is not beautiful, nor wise, nor good, nor powerful as she is. So he seeks petty powers in this place, dominion over those too weak to battle him, riches to flaunt before those he despises. And this does not salve his raw jealousy. Vengeance he must have, against one who has done him only good."

"And when did your talisman vanish?" prompted the old man.

"A month has passed since my father set sail for the Far Islands to attend to his business there. The Cat was within its case of carven wood. Yet four days agone I opened the little doors and set my hand within, and it was not there. None has the key but I, and I believed that my father thought it only a trinket or a keepsake, such as a foolish girl might treasure. So great is the fear of his servants, I doubt that they would steal, even from one whom he keeps prisoner. In all places open to me I have searched, and in despair I have at last sought your aid."

Kla-Noh rose painfully to his feet and struggled up the incline below her. Staring up into her eyes, he said, "You have given this burden to me. Let me now bear it, and keep yourself free for other things. You have power, even without the talisman. Exercise it then, as a gymnast strengthens his muscles. Your father is not here. Good. That gives you the time and the leisure for work. Despair saps the will and the spirit. Discard it as an unworthy thing. Focus your attention upon your arts and bring them to the fullness of fruition. Then, should I succeed, you will be doubly armed. Should I fail, you will have greater strength than you would have done had you despaired alone."

She peered through the deepening gloom, seeing only his small shape black against the darkness. "Old man, I will," she said. "You are wise and clever. Do you seek the Cat; I will seek other things. Together we will thwart Tro-Ven."

* * *

For a day and a night Kla-Noh sat upon his terrace, looking across the Purple Waters. Si-Lun waited in silence, knowing his companion's inscrutable methods. Once they sailed across the bay, lighted by one waxing moon, Ralias, and stood off the cliff shore by the house of Tro-Ven. High in the ranks of tall windows blackly watching the bay, one window glowed with a strange and flickering luminescence. Then, though Si-Lun could not see the smile on the face of his friend, he could hear a smile in his voice as he said, "Ah, she is at work. Let us go home, Si-Lun, and begin our own."

But what he began was not apparent. No mysterious messenger came or went. No stealthy footfall was heard in the night. None who watched the house would have suspected that the old Seeker was frantically busy with his part of the project. Only one who could mark the pigeon's flight could have learned of his working. But his dovecote was an old pastime, and none who knew him had ever learned that it was his communication line to the world of secrets.

When a week had passed, the old man summoned Si-Lun and asked that his craft be made ready for a voyage of several days.

"We will approach rough coastlines and berth in unpeopled coves, so provide for all our wants. No man shall know when we leave or when we return, for when we sail away at moonset another craft shall be moored in the place of this, and our quiet lives will continue, so far as any watcher can discern."

The younger man's eyes glowed with excitement, though he spoke softly. "It begins, then?"

"We go to consult an . . . oracle," said Kla-Noh. "I suspect that I know the answer to my questions, but we must know certainly. There is a spot in the wild, Si-Lun, my friend, which I know of old. I strongly suspect that it is a place where the veil is thin, or there is a hidden door, or a passage exists between this world and that of Li-Ah's mother. I have before now consulted there with voices from the air and the earth, and their words have always been truthful and wise. Only there may we find the track of the Cat with the Sapphire Eyes.

"For I have made inquiry among the high and the low,

the subtle and the crafty, and none among the men of
Shar-Nuhn has pilfered that talisman."

"Then we shall leave at moonset," said Si-Lun, "for the
craft has been provisioned and prepared these two days.
Somewhat do I, also, know of the ways of the Seeker."
And he grinned in his hollow-cheeked way.

At moonset their dark sail merged with the dark sky as
they slid from the bay into the full current of the Purple
Waters.

Within two days they sighted a grim cape, thrusting its
shoulder into boiling waves amid tumbled boulders.
Standing well off, they rounded its profile and hove to in
a steep-sided cove, then waited for darkness.

When the full moon and the waning one were the only
light left in the sky, the two Seekers paddled to the shore
and found a perilous path that led through young growth
upward toward the lip of the circling cliff.

Though Kla-Noh affected the infirmities of age, when
pressed by need he moved with the ease of a young man.
Long before moonset the two reached the meadows that
topped the cliffs and moved along a line of pines toward
a distant wood.

"There," whispered Kla-Noh, "lies the place of the oracle. This is my greatest secret, and I have had no son to
share it. You are my spirit's son, and this is my bequest to
you, for with this you have the answer to any question
unanswerable by other means."

"This is a great gift," said Si-Lun softly. "You have
taken me, who had no home and no father, and have
given me both. It is enough. Yet with this you have given
me a life of ease and honor. Be certain, I will use it well,
O Seeker."

The wood glowed dimly in moonlight as they approached. No night bird sang, no current of air moved

the branches. They entered and moved along a faint path that their feet felt, though their eyes could not see. So quietly did they move, and in such an enchanted stillness, that when Kla-Noh paused, his companion felt that he had been waked from a dream. But the old man was busy with the pack Si-Lun carried, feeling among its contents for a bundle of herbs, and a fagot of wood and his heat stone. When his torch was lit at last, a fragrance moved with them along the path and into a circle of stones and giant trees.

At the center of the little amphitheater the Seeker stopped and thrust the torch into a riven pillar that stood there. At once the silence, which had seemed complete, became a thing of agony, pressing into the ears like rods of wax. For a long moment they floated in a bubble of nothingness, then the bubble popped, and they again drew breath. From the air about them came voices, faint yet strong, remote yet so near that they sounded within their skulls.

"We are," they said. "We have been. We shall be. What need have you, young friend?"

Kla-Noh sank to his knees, and Si-Lun covered his ears, that he might not hear the voices, and staggered from the circle until he stumbled upon his own pack, fell, and lay, waiting for his friend.

* * *

The warped fragment of one waning moon hung over the Purple Waters. Under the golden-flowered bush waited Kla-Noh and Si-Lun, apprehensively. Long was twilight done, and the lady had not stepped upon the terrace. For hours they had crouched in their pollened lair, debating whether to go or to risk approaching the house by stealth.

But at last a lagging step was heard, and a voice said hopelessly to the air, "One day is left before my father's return. Where are my friends? Have I a friend? Or am I doomed to work the destruction of all I love?"

Then Kla-Noh rose up and said, "We are here, Lady. And despair you need not, though the Cat with the Sapphire Eyes will not be seen again in this world."

"It is gone, then, irretrievably?" she asked mournfully.

"It has returned to its maker," said the old man sternly. "Long have I known your mother's people, though I did not know who they were. Through a way I found long ago I have spoken with your mother herself, though hard and long the task must be to reach the ear of a queen. No man stole away the Cat with the Sapphire Eyes, that I learned soon. Then I thought long. Your father, though subtle and powerful, still could not reach across the sea— as yet—to remove it from your care. But your mother, if my speculations were not in error, was able to do this thing.

"You are about to ask why. But think. You have taught your only child the old strengths you know. You have loved her and nurtured her, but she will be taken into a strange world by an enemy whom she must fight alone. She is untried in her arts, utterly unused to battle with sorcerers. She will need, above all things, confidence. So you create a talisman. But you are able to see into that world where she is taken, and you find that she is relying upon that talisman to the injury of her powers. You know she has more than she will need of art and of will, if she will only use them, practice with them, strengthen them. So you reach out your thought, and you take back the talisman. For such is your confidence in your child that you have no fear of her failure.

"Do you see, child?"

The lady swayed tiredly upon the edge of the terrace. "I see," she said clearly. "In my unwisdom, I misused it. And in your wisdom, you made me learn to work without it. And tomorrow my father will return to find an enemy within his own stronghold, ready to wrest from him his stolen arts and to thwart his twisted schemes.

"My thanks, friends, for your aid. Without it, much that is good might have perished." They saw the slim shadows that were her hands, and each took one and touched it to his forehead, and they turned and went into their craft and sailed away.

And when, under a red and raddled moon of the next night, the house of Tro-Ven sank upon its crumbled buttresses and heaved, amid a shower of strange lights, into the sea, they watched from afar, sitting upon their terrace. When the grinding crash had ended, they reached out their hands to each other and clasped them tightly.

"May the gods grant," said Kla-Noh, "that the lady has found her way home."

III

The Man Who Thought Batwise

Si-Lun and Kla-Noh sat upon their terrace, gazing across the Purple Waters at the far side of the Bay of Shar-Nuhn. Just visible in the evening light was a jumble of fallen stone that marred the neat shoreline.

"And there stood the house of Tro-Ven, merchant lord and warlock," said Kla-Noh sardonically.

"Such seems the fate of those who seek to overcome the limitations of mankind," answered Si-Lun. "One other such have I known, and his fate was stranger—though not, perhaps, more unexpected—than that of yonder departed wizard."

Kla-Noh's eyebrows rose in an arc of surprise. "Never before have you spoken of your past," he said. "And though I am a Seeker After Secrets I have never sought beyond your willingness to reveal. But surely, now, you have a tale to tell me, and I am anxious to hear."

And this is the story told by Si-Lun:

* * *

Across the Purple Waters, many months' voyage beyond the Far Islands, lies a vast continent whose forbidding mountains, clothed in forests of fir and pine, hide valleys of the utmost fertility and cities of amazing splendor. In the deeps of those mountains I was born and grew to be a youth. And when the time had come for me to learn a trade, my father sought in the greatest city for a master who might appreciate and bring to fruition the talents of Si-Lun, his only son, for even then I was adept at ferreting out things hidden and things forgotten.

Though I longed for the life of a seafarer, my father was adamant. My fortune would be made, did I but apply myself and please the master he chose. So he apprenticed me to Lo-Vahr, Doctor of the Sciences and Investigator of the Unknown, and I was sent to live in his tall house which, though of utmost luxury, was placed most strangely in the narrow streets of the oldest part of the city of Am-Brak.

Seldom, I should surmise, was there an apprentice who loved his master. Never, I'd wager, was there one who more heartily despised his than did I. Lo-Vahr was a narrow man—in body, face, eyes, and mind. For though he sought to know that which was unknown, he had no real interest in what he learned. Only for the furtherance of his plots and machinations did he seek, not for the discovery of the truth and the straightening of tangled lives and purposes.

I was young, very young, and Truth was the goddess I worshiped. How I despised that one-dimensioned man who would not respect her, but used her as he would a trull!

The missions upon which I was sent did not increase my liking for him. Into squalid tenements I went, seeking filthy crones who bartered stinking bundles for my master's coin. Only once did I investigate such a burden, and never again for years. The hag who provided it had bitten the good gold coin that my master had sent to her, then had looked me in the eyes with such a mocking and leering glint in her own that, as soon as I was out of sight in the higgledy-piggledy alleys, I opened the wrapping and peered into the box I carried. It contained a newborn child; I think it had been strangled. I left the good meal I had eaten in that alley, and never again, until I had learned a purpose of my own, did I seek to know what it was I was transporting.

Necromancy was some part of what Lo-Vahr practiced, though I doubt that he was an adept at that, or at anything. Alchemy he dabbled in, without success. I found, indeed, that his reputation was based upon his mysterious demeanor and great wealth, which he had from his fathers, and not from any effort that he put forth. He needed no apprentice, for he had nothing to teach. Only for a messenger did he have need.

So for three years I trudged through slimy alleys and into night-bound burial grounds, seeking for things I would not think of for purposes I did not wish to know.

The familiarity of daily contact dulls perception. For how many months a gradual change in my master had been taking place I cannot tell, but one evening it was brought forcibly to my attention.

It was my duty to stand behind his chair at the evening meal and to keep his glass filled and his needs satisfied. Upon the evening in question, I was more alert than usual, for Lo-Vahr had guests, one a lovely young girl who was the daughter of an agent whom he was entertaining.

During the meal he flattered the father and watched the girl, and I watched him, thinking, "How strangely bent he has grown, and how pointed his ears. Hunching his thick shoulders forward and bending his head as he speaks, he looks like nothing so much as a bat."

And as I thought this, he turned his head and looked

me in the eyes, gesturing for me to fill his glass, which was by no means empty. The glance he gave me was like a hot needle through all my nerves, bringing me to full alertness. Though I hurried to do his bidding, my faculties were focused upon the meaning that those slitted black eyes had conveyed.

Narrowly I observed him then, noticing the accumulation of oddities that had settled upon him like a pall of dust. As he escorted his guests from the hall, he took the arm of the young girl, and in his black cloak, with his thin arm crooked and his stooping shape turned to her, I could see nothing save an enormous bat. The girl felt something of the same aura, for she shuddered from head to foot and then apologized in a frightened manner.

When it grew late and the guests took their leave, I went about lighting the night lamps and checking the bolts of the house doors. As I drew near the chamber of Lo-Vahr, a strange compulsion came upon me. I moved noisily past his door and down the curving stair. Then I crept back up, slipped behind the heavy garnet curtains that covered the windows at the stair head, and stepped out onto the ledge that circled the second floor of the house.

His window was faintly lighted. Crouching on the narrow ledge, I peered cautiously in, risking only one eye's width past the window edge. Then I froze in the darkness, attempting to melt into the chilly stone of the wall. Lo-Vahr stood at the window, arms spread wide to grip the frame, head tilted back, as if he watched the sky. But his room was firelit and the sky was dark—what could he have seen?

To me he was a dark shape against the orange glow. It was then I noted that he had taken to having his cloak cut out into points at the hem, like to the wings of a bat.

And then, above me in the night sky, I heard a chittering of many shrill cries and felt about my back the swift brushing of passing wings.

Abandoning caution, I retreated along the ledge and into the window from which I had come. But I was not seen. He was communing with his familiars.

Then did I watch him indeed! So used was he to my presence that he seldom noticed me. It was possible for me to observe his comings and goings, his visitors and his expeditions into the old city. And I found ways to watch him even when he locked himself away into his chambers. For the attics above were untenanted and capacious, and it was simple work for a youngling to find the way to those above his apartments and to make peepholes in well-chosen places.

Of his disgusting rites I will not speak. The thought that I had carried the . . . ingredients . . . for them through the streets in my hands made me quease. But there was a dreadful consistency in his incantations, and a sort of diverse similarity in the things he used in his spells, that spoke of a single, focused purpose.

Being young, I was without strong moral scruples in things of this kind. I knew, certainly, that the Initiates in the Towers of Truth taught that this work was all that was evil and corrupting. I watched, nonetheless, with no thought of thwarting him, but my old affinity for secrets led me to learn what I could.

More of my time was now taken up with his odious errands, but I examined the things I bore and noted them upon a tablet which I kept faithfully. Also did I note his words and motions as he made his private magics, to puzzle over their possible purpose in the deeps of the night when I could not sleep.

Often he invited the agent and his daughter to the evening meal, and the women servants began to whisper in the halls and kitchens that the master must be intending to take a bride. Attentive he was, but not, it seemed to me, in the way of a suitor. And the conversations between the father and my master began to have strange undercurrents, almost like—haggling?

The girl grew pale and thin, and I knew her to be afraid, though we never exchanged any word. Then I began to have an inkling of my master's course, perhaps of his ultimate purpose.

I believe that the girl's intuition led her to much the same conclusions that I reached, so far as her part in the program was concerned. And being young, I was also chivalrous. I determined to protect her if it might be done, and to avenge her if it could not.

Thus it was that I decided upon a bold course. There was in the newer city an Adept of science and sorcery, well respected by the Initiates and feared by the petty warlocks and practitioners of unclean arts. He was removed from evil, but not sworn to expose any who came to him with unorthodox problems. To him I went, bearing my tablet of notes and my strange tale.

At the door of his modest house I almost lost courage. He was indeed a great man in the city of Am-Brak and in the country. Why should he concern himself with the troubles of an apprentice? Yet I knocked, and to the servant told my name and that I was the apprentice of a warlock in the city, not naming him.

After a time that seemed long, the servant returned and beckoned. I followed her down a white-paneled hall into a low room filled with light and warmth that radiated from a dazzling globe set into a niche in the wall. So absorbed was I in trying to puzzle out its mode of operation that I almost missed seeing the sturdy old man who walked forward and looked at me piercingly.

"You are Si-Lun," he said. "And who is Si-Lun, and why does he seek En-Bir?"

I started, then recollected myself and bowed. "Si-Lun is a lowly person with an uncommon tale to tell, though I must not name names other than my own. Here"—and I proffered my notes—"is a tablet filled with observations of rites practiced by my master. Greatly do I need to know where they are leading and if"—I looked up at him uneasily—"if they might mean harm to any human being."

His gray eyes sparked and his brow crinkled as he motioned me to a chair and sat down with my tablet upon his knees. Long he perused it, turning back at times to read again bits at the beginning. When he turned to question me, he seemed to know my answers before I made them.

When he was satisfied, he leaned back before the bright globe and sighed deeply. "This is a heavy matter you have brought to me," he said. "You are right, by moral laws if not by the laws of apprenticeship, to question the aims of these practices. For the rites that you have shown to me culminate"—he looked at me narrowly —"in the murder of a virgin."

I trust I did not blanch. I nodded and said, "Such was my conclusion, though I hoped that I was in error. Yet I cannot, by the rules of honor and of apprenticeship, reveal my master's name to you, that you may put an end to his works. What can I do to make this evil turn to good, and to save the unlucky wench he has chosen?"

Then that great man leaned forward and spoke, and I listened, and when he was done I bowed and kissed his hand and went away to my own place.

In a week it was known in the house that there would be a guest to stay, and the maids giggled in the halls as they made up a set of rooms in the same hall as my master's. I listened with contempt to their scandalous gossiping, thinking how far better it would be if Lo-Vahr had only designs upon her virtue.

There was great feasting upon the night that little Ne-La came to stay in the house of Lo-Vahr. The great wheels of candles were lit in the state chamber, and fires were set to burning in the cavernous fireplaces. But the only guests were Ne-La and her father, and when the father went, the lights were all put out and the house stood in darkness.

Then Lo-Vahr sent for me and, in a voice taut with urgency, said, "This night you go upon your most important errand for me. In the street of the Crane, in the house of At-Nah, you will find one who waits with a parcel ready. Give her this bag of coins and hurry back with your burden. This is of great import. Go, and return with utmost speed."

So I hurried out and made my way with all speed to the appointed place. But when I had the bundle, I went first to the Tower of Truth that stood in the old city and knocked upon the door. To the attendant I said, "I must see an Initiate. I am the one sent by En-Bir, the Adept."

The Initiate came at once and took my bundle from me. Into an interior room he took it, and I could hear him chanting in the high language of the Initiates, and I could smell strange fragrances. But when he returned it to me, it was just as it had been.

The Initiate looked me full in the face and said, "It is a responsibility heavy for one so young that you have been given. Strong thoughts and good will go with you, to strengthen your spirit and steady your hands. Your apprenticeship is at an end, though you may not yet know it. When you feel that you are free, return here, and we will find a way"—and here he smiled—"to find you a berth upon an honest ship, that you may have your heart's desire."

As I hurried away, back to the house of Lo-Vahr, I was consumed with wonder. How had the Initiate known my secret wish? Never had I mentioned it to En-Bir. Certainly they were wonderful men, but their ways were mysterious and fearsome.

I returned well within the time set by my master, for so smoothly had the extra time been spent that it cost me only a little effort at speed to recover the lost minutes.

Lo-Vahr waited at the door of his chambers, looking now and again down the hall toward the closed door of Ne-La's rooms. When he heard my step, he turned, and his cloak spread in the draft, so that a bat, in truth, stood with claw outstretched. I placed the bundle in that awful hand and turned and fled down the stair.

Now was the hardest of all disciplines mine to learn. I must wait, hoping, believing that the rites of the Initiate would render the thing that my master would use to begin his ritual destructive to him. Yet I stole back and hid behind the garnet curtains. Should all fail, I would still try to save the girl, No-La.

In my heart I pictured my master drawing his foul diagrams upon his hearth, setting out the tools of his spell. His eyes would be glittering, I knew, with his awful lust, not for a woman, but for the ability to fly like a bat.

Strange, is it not, that so childish a desire should devour a man in his prime, to his utter corruption?

I learned waiting, and dreading, and prayer, in that

short time which seemed so long. But beside my heart I felt the presence of the Initiate's promise, and it warmed me from despair.

Faintly I could hear Lo-Vahr's chanting and the clinking of vessels as he moved them. More faintly I could hear Ne-La's steps as she paced nervously in her rooms. But above all there hung a pall of dark silence, a waiting, airless miasma of stillness.

I leaned back in the embrasure of the window, and my eye was caught by a blur of motion. Making a frame of my hands, I peered out and saw by starlight a cloud of bats that whirled and boiled about the house of Lo-Vahr. I opened the window and leaned far out. His window glowed with fitful light, and I knew that his fire burned high.

Then, on the wall of the adjoining house, I saw his shadow appear as he moved toward the window. Arms spread wide, cloak drooping like bat wings, he seemed to stagger, and I heard a terrible cry.

There was a growing red glare from the fire, which seemed to have caught the room. I turned and leaped from the window space to the door of Ne-La.

"The house is burning!" I cried. "Come to safety!"

Never had she heard my voice, but she knew it was not his and came at once. Sending her down the stair, I went to the servants' wing and cried a warning to them, then hurried after Ne-La, but she had fled into the night and, I hope and believe, to some place of safety unrelated to a father who would sell her to a warlock.

I sought for her for a time as the firelight grew behind me. Then I turned and looked a last time upon the house of Lo-Vahr. It was a tower of flame. I could see the ragged line of servants straggling from the wide door. The window of Lo-Vahr was upon the other side, but I could see a sprinkling of specks against the light that I knew to be the bats, and I could hear their cries as they fled the heat down the dark alleys. Then I knew that I was indeed free, and I went to the Tower of Truth.

So I became a seaman and lost for a time my love of secret things, and for all time any desire to look into the ways of warlocks.

IV

Shallah Sits at Her Loom

A curving wing of shadow raced across the Bay of Shar-Nuhn, dyeing the Purple Waters with dapplings of darkness. High in his pigeon loft, Kla-Noh, Seeker After Secrets, watched with delight as the spectrum of color spread below him. The softly muttering pigeons supplied a quiet music to suit his mood, and he felt his heart lift as he saw, far to the south, a belated bird speeding its way toward his loft.

Swiftly as a cloud it came, and it alighted and entered its nook with a weary air.

"Well, old friend," said Kla-Noh, "long has it been since you last rested in my aerie. Now what has brought you winging from the south?"

He lifted the bird, feeling its throbbing life hot between his hands as he soothed and fondled it. From its leg he took the small container that bore the message, then he hurried down the steps to his sitting room. To his reading table the old Seeker went at once.

Si-Lun, entering from the terrace, lighted the lamp for his foster father, and the two sat side by side, studying the coded symbols inscribed upon the tiny bit of paper.

"Strange," said Kla-Noh. "From Lo-Shel, who lives in the mountain fastnesses to the south, has the bird come.

Always have I sought word from Lo-Shel, never he from me. Quiet are his ways and his life; strong is his mind, and great his heart. No trouble—and he has known many, living as he does upon the very edge of the lands of men—has ever thwarted his abilities. What can he need of me?"

Slowly he deciphered the message contained in the crabbed symbols. Si-Lun bent closer to see as the words formed, one by one, upon the page beneath the Seeker's pen. " 'Shallah sits at her loom,' " he read. "Shallah?"

"Wife and heart's heart to Lo-Shel. Seer and prophet is she, and many other things, yet tender to him and to their children and strong in any adversity." Kla-Noh thumbed through a worn tablet, seeking for the symbol keys, then wrote again: "She does not speak, though the younglings cry at her side. She will not eat. She falls at night across the loom and must be carried to her couch. She looks always at the weave, with horror in her eyes. Come to me, my friend. I have great need."

The two Seekers looked each into the other's eyes. They nodded, slowly, and Si-Lun rose from his chair. "We go by sea or by land?" he asked. "Steep are the anchorages to the far south, yet few are the roads. How go you when you visit Lo-Shel?"

"We must obtain riding beasts. Send Nu-Veh into Shar-Nuhn after supplies, for we will be many days upon the road. Go you to the farm yonder after beasts, and I shall send a winged courier to assure Lo-Shel that we come."

Swiftly could the Seekers move when there was need, and morning saw them upon the road, mounted upon the sturdy beasts that their neighbor had supplied. Late summer lit the fields with gold upon either hand, and they rode with enjoyment in the balmy air, keeping a steady gait yet never forcing their mounts.

Two days they rode before the mountains rose, a dim blue line across the southern horizon. From the warm comfort of their way they could see, glinting in the sunlight, peaks wrapped in never-melting snows.

"There lies the first pass that we must cross," said Kla-Noh, pointing. "It is well that it is summer, for in winter the passes lie buried beneath terrible masses of snow. Even now it will be a perilous journey which, without the aid of these strong mounts, might well leave our bones upon those heights with those of many other wayfarers."

But their pace did not slacken, and as day followed day they came upon the ragged hills that were the outriders of the ranges beyond. As they mounted into the heights, they found a chill growing in the air, and soon they needed the warm clothing that Nu-Veh had packed for them. And still they went up, following roads that were narrow shelves which twisted their ways up the walls of gorges beside rills of singing water. Great trees overarched their way, bracing green-furred arms across the cold blueness of sky and digging strong toes into the scanty soil between outcroppings of stone.

"Almost," said Si-Lun, when they had paused to rest the animals, "almost this seems as my birthplace upon the Far Continent. There stand mountains fit to pierce the sky, forests such as these, green waters falling from stone. The sly beasts peering at us from their coverts might be those which I hunted in my youth. This seems a journey into the past."

"Lo-Shel is to be thanked," answered Kla-Noh, "for bringing us out into this world of strong stillness. Study and song are well, in their place, yet I would not miss the joy of testing my skill and my will against these uncaring fastnesses."

Then they went up again, and up, until the clouds

closed around their heads and stopped their vision. Yet
they moved along the tenuous trails, which now were
closed in on either hand by rocky cliffs whose tops were
hidden in the drifting mists. They crossed the pass before
evening and moved again downward into fir-green valleys.

For more than a week they journeyed thus, doggedly
challenging passes clogged with snow, invisible with
cloud, perilous with loosened stones. They grew thin, and
their beasts also. Altitude and effort took their toll of en-
ergy and flesh. But there came an afternoon when they
descended a twisting track upon the side of a great beast
of a mountain and saw, across a little valley enclosed on
all sides by forested ridges, a column of smoke rising in
the still, chill air.

"There," said Kla-Noh, halting his panting mount, "is
the house of Lo-Shel. Soon we will shelter again within
walls, for which the gods be thanked."

The valley through which they rode was narrow, following a stream that ran swiftly over a rocky course.
Upon either side of the water they could see tilled fields
and meadows where kine grazed upon the late-summer
grasses. Hands had been busy drawing life from the soil
and the plants and the waters. Soon they could see byres
for the cattle and tall barns for the winter's store of hay,
which was standing ready for the blade. Yet no human
form could they see, though the sun was not over the
ridge to the west and some hours of light were left in the
day.

The house of Lo-Shel stood at the end of a lane lined
with flowering trees, which had dropped their rosy petals
into the track. So the two Seekers walked up a way
strewn with blossoms, leaving their beasts to graze

among the grasses by the roadside. Only the chimney smoke spoke of the presence of living beings, for the windows were blank and no welcoming face looked from the panes of the door.

As Kla-Noh's tap sounded through the rooms, there came a sudden susurrus of voices, hushed exclamations, then the clicking of feet upon stone flags. The heavy door opened, and a small face looked up at them from just over waist height. Round blue eyes grew rounder, and the little maid lifted her skirts and said, with a matronly air, "Come in, good sirs. My father is within, and I shall call him if you will but wait in the sitting room."

She scurried out of sight down the passage, and the two Seekers smiled as they sat in comfort, awaiting her return. Instead there came a heavier tread, and Lo-Shel himself hurried into the room. His weathered face wore the print of care as he took Kla-Noh's proffered hands and said, "Little did I think that you could arrive so soon, my friend. Heavy has been the burden of life these past weeks, and only the promise of your help has given me hope for the present or the future. But you are weary and must rest. Li-Tha! No-Ri! Come and show the Seekers to their chamber, that they may wash and refresh themselves before the evening meal."

When they had satisfied their host that their comforts had been well attended, Si-Lun and Kla-Noh sat with Lo-Shel privately in his chamber and asked of his trouble.

"This is a strange malady which has stricken my Shallah," he sighed. "You know that she has ever been a seer of the future and the past and has many a time woven at her loom in a trance, to find that her weaving depicts events of the faraway and the near at hand, that which has been and that which is to be. Often has she wept bitterly that the things she has woven must prove to be true, yet she is wise and strong and always has she conquered her grief. Over the past years the trance loomings had waned until she had begun to hope that the burden had been lifted from her. Happy was she as I have seldom seen her, and the house rang with her song and laughter, and the children bloomed in the blessed light of her cheer. Our life was joyful as never before, and all seemed clear as a summer sky.

"The ending of the spring brought a change. Through the early summer she remained in good cheer, yet she seemed to be ever listening to something faraway, something that she could not quite hear. At midsummer, suddenly in the night she rose from our couch and went to her loom. Though her eyes were open, yet I could see that she neither heard nor saw that which was before her. She did not change the colors but set at once to weaving, looking with dread at the strange patterns that emerged in the cloth.

"Long did I watch, studying the runes, but none save she can decipher them. I returned to our couch, but did not sleep, and through the long night I could hear the thumping of the loom. I lay in dread, for I had seen that in her eyes which never had been there before. Not until the next night did she fall at the loom, and I carried her to bed and forced milk between her lips. And thus have I done for all the weeks since, though I know not how she walks to the loom of a morning, when she has eaten nothing except that which we can coax her to swallow in sleep. She sleeps now, for the hours when she can sit and weave grow fewer each day, and she falls into slumber before the sun sets."

Kla-Noh leaned forward and laid his hand upon the

man's knee. "Be comforted, old friend. What we can do will be done. Long have I lived amid strange secrets and unearthly matters. Mayhap there will be among my recollections one that will work the cure for your beloved Shallah."

Si-Lun also leaned forward. "Not so wise or so old as Kla-Noh am I, yet I, too, have traveled far and seen much of the ways of other places than this. Surely we may manage, between us, relief for your helpmeet."

"Let me, then, take you to her, that you may look upon her in sleep. She will not awaken until dawn, whatever the disturbance within her chamber. Perhaps you may see some sign that my anxiety has caused my eyes to miss."

The red light of sunset lay across the couch where Shallah lay, and the color gave her slender face the flush of health. Yet Kla-Noh, touching her forehead and her wrist, felt a chill in her flesh, and the pulsing of blood through her wrist was light and rapid. There were blue shadows about her eyes, and her small frame was worn away to the light bones. The Seeker felt a chill in his own frame as he summed up her state.

He turned to Lo-Shel and said, "In my pack there is a box that contains a powder. We shall add that to her milk and soup. It will strengthen her body, though it will not aid her spirit. Yet we must keep that spirit burning in this frail flesh, if we are to give it help. We shall think long this night, Lo-Shel, on this matter."

Then the two Seekers went to their chamber and talked long as night drew in. Yet no similar sickness had either seen, in all their varied experiences.

Morning found the house of Lo-Shel a hive of activity as the four sons and three daughters of the family accom-

plished their forenoon tasks. After breakfast all went into
the fields, for the hay was ripe for harvest. Only Lo-Shel
remained behind with the Seekers.

"We have propped her in our arms and spooned milk
between her lips," he said to Kla-Noh. "Soon now she will
awaken and, if I am not by to wrap her in her housegown
and place slippers upon her feet, she will go in her night-
robe to the loom and begin to spin. Come with me and
watch."

So Si-Lun and Kla-Noh watched outside the chamber
door while Lo-Shel dressed Shallah. Then the door
opened and she stepped swiftly, surely, yet blindly down
the passageway to the loom chamber, where she sat at
once and began weaving.

Pressing treadle, throwing shuttle, swinging batten
with hypnotic rhythm, she seemed weaving the cycles of
time and of life into the growing web before her. Her
eyes were set upon the pattern, her mind faraway—or inward. No touch reached her consciousness, no word pene-
trated her ear. All her being was focused upon the warp,
the weft upon the loom. When Si-Lun stepped forward
and grasped her hands, preventing their motion, she
writhed as if in agony, her eyes still fixed, past his shoulder, upon the cloth.

The men retreated into the passageway, their faces
grave and their hearts filled with foreboding.

"Let us go into the fields," said Kla-Noh, "and work in
the hay with the others, clearing our minds and relieving
our hearts with good labor. Too much thought stifles itself, and to stretch the muscles oftentimes stretches the
ability to think."

Good was the clean air, fragrant the cut hay as they
walked in the fields, forking the layers over to dry in the

sun. A spatter of insects shot up before their feet with a crackle of wings, and the sweat ran down their arms and their backs, cooling them in the breezes.

In the next field the children were scything the standing grasses, shouting and laughing as they disturbed nesting birds and sunning serpents. The air rang with birdsong from the surrounding forest, and the stream added its clear note among the stones of its bed. The little valley among the mountains seemed brimful with all the good things of living, and the spirits of the Seekers rose, even in the midst of their worry.

"The gods will not spoil this paradise with tragedy," said Si-Lun, pausing to wipe the sweat from his face upon his sleeve. "They have placed here all that is good and given it to those who know it and prize it and nurture it as best they may. Surely they have also sent us for a purpose and with an answer to the darkness that threatens."

"The answer will come," said Kla-Noh, leaning upon his fork and gazing up into the ridges that shone with fir-dark and gold in the morning sunlight. "A sureness grows within me. We bear the answer in our hearts and our hands. It but remains to seek it out. In this place nothing is impossible, nothing insoluble. We were sent, and we are here. For the present, this is enough."

At midday all returned to the house, where the thumping of the loom continued, regular as the pounding of waves upon a shore. The food was sweet in their mouths, and they worked the afternoon away with zest, feeling their muscles rejoicing in their strength and their lungs expanding in the fir-sharp air.

As they went, washed and cleanly clothed, to their supper, Si-Lun said quietly to his foster father, "It may be that a solution is knocking at the door of my consciousness. In some cranny of my memory there is a stored fact that is now tapping away, seeking to be refound and brought into the light."

Kla-Noh squeezed his arm and smiled. "When we have eaten and the younglings are about their evening sports, then we will talk of this."

Thus, when the children went out into the twilight to play upon the lawns and in the edges of the forest, they sought out Lo-Shel and sat with him in quietude, lending their presence as Si-Lun thought long.

"What, Lo-Shel, is the use to which Shallah puts the cloth that is spun in her trances?" he asked at last.

"It is folded away and put into a chest, which she never opens save to add more," he answered. "She seems to fear to look upon it, yet she lifts it with caution and tenderly packs it away. I have never touched it, though never has she said me nay. It seems to me such a mystery that I am wary of it."

Si-Lun nodded. A wrinkle formed between his green eyes. "Has she never ripped out the weave?"

Lo-Shel almost blanched. "Nay, never. Such would seem almost . . . blasphemy. It is sent of the gods."

"True," the Seeker answered. "Yet this sending will end by slaying Shallah, as surely as sunrise. So we must act in unorthodox ways to break it and to bring her back into the world of life. It is in my thought that such has been done before, in another time and place, with another kind of sending altogether. Yet the principle is the same. If we destroy the thing whole, it might rebound against Shallah. But if we simply . . . unmake it, there is a hope that she may return unscathed. Will you give your leave for us to try this?"

"Truly I will," said Lo-Shel. "I will unweave the cloth with my own hand if such will save my wife from this doom."

"You must be there, hale and strong, to welcome her back," said Kla-Noh. "The unweaving is work for Seekers. We have striven with strange things before and may protect ourselves in ways unknown to you."

The powder added to her food had given Shallah more than usual endurance, and still she sat at the loom. They entered the chamber, and Lo-Shel took his place behind her. Then Si-Lun approached the loom, with Kla-Noh close beside him. And when Shallah sank in sleep before the stilled heckles, the two Seekers began pulling out the weft that she had woven. Tedious work it was, and difficult for their clumsy fingers, yet they persisted, and the patterns began to disappear.

Then Shallah gave a great cry and sought to raise herself, but Lo-Shel held her in his arms and would not let her go. Thread after thread was loosened. The light grew dim and Kla-Noh brought candles, yet still they worked, ripping from the loom the long belt of cloth woven by Shallah over weeks and months. At first she struggled wildly, but as the patterns melted away she grew quiet. And still they tugged and pulled and cut and ripped.

At last Lo-Shel whispered, "Her eyes—her eyes are beginning to see."

And so it was. The blue eyes that had stared so blindly now began to shift their gaze away from that ill-omened cloth. A puzzled wrinkle crossed her forehead, and Shallah looked up at her husband, who held her closely.

Into the night, long and long, the Seekers worked, and before day the weaving was reduced to a great mound of yarn that eddied about their feet and stuck upon their clothing. Then Shallah smiled at them, the smile of a weary child, and drooped in sleep upon Lo-Shel's shoulder.

Then they went away into their own chambers and closed the doors and slept, while the sun rejoiced the mountains, and the birds and the children greeted the renewal of the day.

V

The Weatherwitch

A wrack of cloud, black and swollen with wind, boiled above Shar-Nuhn, and the Purple Waters, from the uttermost reaches of their domain, sent tall waves thundering to hurtle against the bar sheltering the bay. And the bay itself seethed and spit like a witch's caldron, sending sheeting spray across the terrace of Kla-Noh, the Seeker, to rattle in volleys against his walls and his shutters.

Inside, all was warmth and light, and Si-Lun read aloud from one of the old heroic poets, against the fitting backdrop of the wind, as Kla-Noh touched his harp from time to time, when the outward clamor paused for breath.

When Si-Lun reached the stanza that said:

And the galloping horses of the north were loosed in the
    heavens,
rending cloud apart, loosing the stones in the mountains,
snorting into the lands of men, to their utter
    desolation . . .

a veritable tumult of wind and water hurled itself against the seaward walls, and no sound save the warring elements could be heard. The stone house could not shake, but so great was the sound of the storm that both Seekers felt shaken to their souls, and they looked at one another with wonder.

"Houses will fall and ships will sail into the halls of the gods this night," said Kla-Noh when, at last, it eased. "Many years have I stood upon this earth, yet until now I have met no such storm as this."

Si-Lun nodded. "Long years I was a son of the sea," he said. "Storms were my meat and rocked my hammock, yet this is no storm of my experience. But, more than this, a question worries at my heart, Kla-Noh. Such a tempest will wreak dreadful woe upon the fleets of Shar-Nuhn. For such an event was the First Secret of Shar-Nuhn discovered, and, in the months I have anchored in the port, never has a storm been allowed to do more than blow away the smokes and soots of the town. Know you why the Initiates in the Tower of Truth should allow such devastation?"

His mentor rose and went to the shuttered window, peering sidewise through the louvers at the wash that was his terrace and the blur that was the bay. Turning, he shivered in his green robe and said, "That question has gnawed at my mind for a day and a night, since this unearthly broil began. I agree that it seems no storm of this world. And if the First Secret is powerless to quell it, such it must be, for the Initiates have warded well the seas and the shore since it came into their guardianship. Never would they give over the city to destruction and the sons and the ships of the Shar-Neen to death, if such could in any wise be avoided.

"Long did I move among the secrets of Shar-Nuhn, seeking and selling, and much did I learn of the workings of the First and the Second Secrets of Shar-Nuhn. Of the Third"—and the old man smiled knowingly at his companion—"you know as much as I. In all my probings into the roots of rumor and the basis of knowledge, never did I find a whisper that there might be a limit upon the power of the secrets of Shar-Nuhn. No Initiate of my acquaintance (and I know many and have known many more who have now passed beyond the veil of death) ever intimated that such there might be.

"So enfolded are the Initiates into the fabric of nature and the purposes of the gods that their rule has seemed absolute in the waters and the winds and upon the dry lands. For among them never has there been one man or woman who has sought personal enrichment or undue power over the lives of fellow beings. Living within the law, they have been empowered to use it to shape the ends that seem wise to the wisest of them. So this . . . invasion by the elements"—and Kla-Noh shuddered again—"smells of the unnatural and, perhaps, the evil."

Si-Lun drew his lean shoulders together and nodded. "So it has seemed to me, though, save for the instance that you know, I have never had extensive dealing with the Initiates."

A loosened slate rattled down the roof, and both men started. Before the clatter had stopped, a knock sounded at the door, and the two Seekers looked at each other in utmost astonishment as the servant padded down the passageway to answer the summons.

A howl of wind entered with the visitor, and he stood on the matting, dripping streams of water from his blue robes and his grizzled beard. As the servant helped him to remove his outer robe, the silver symbol worked into the front of his garment shone in the warm light from the room where Kla-Noh waited. Seeing it, both the old Seeker and the young moved into the hallway at once and bowed low before the man who stood there.

Kla-Noh raised his head and said, "Great must be the

need and unprecedented the urgency of your errand, that you, Ru-Anh, should come to me, and on such an afternoon. Far more fitting would it be if you, the Father of Initiates, should send for me to attend you in the Tower of Truth."

"Necessity and the welfare of Shar-Nuhn have brought me to your door, my friend," said the Initiate grimly, shaking the worst of the water from his beard and striding into the warm sitting room, where he stood before the fire and began to steam slightly as the wet evaporated from his clothing.

"For these two days we have striven with the waters and the winds, struggling with our utmost power to ease the fury of this tempest. Yet while those of us who are concerned with such were battling, others of our order were at work in their own ways, seeking into the causes and the roots and the workings of the storm. For well we knew that this is no simple matter of up-currents and warm and cold bodies of air.

"Today one of the wisest of our Seekers into the Spirit was interrupted in her trance—was swept from it, in fact, into a maelstrom of foreign emotion and turmoil such as she had never before encountered. Only with the aid of two of her strongest associates was she enabled to control the flow of feeling and to explore it, seeking back and back along the current of hatred and anger until she found—dimly, it is true—a source and a cause. We believe that it may well be a true finding, and we also believe that you have some knowledge of the matter or of the person who caused the madness of despair that is at the root of this disaster."

His host raised his brows, and Si-Lun opened his mouth to speak, then thought better of it and nodded instead.

Ru-Anh surveyed them both. "Ah, you have a suspicion, I see. It is well. Nu-Rea, our Seeker into the Spirit, found at the limit of her seeking one who sought the destruction of Shar-Nuhn with all her soul and spirit. For one of ours has injured her, how we do not yet know, in a terrible way, and because of Tro-Ven, merchant of Shar-Nuhn, she is now compassing our destruction. We cannot ask Tro-Ven for an accounting, for he is, as you know, gathered to his fathers. Yet in his downfall we were aware that Kla-Noh, the Seeker After Secrets, was not idle. Never have you sought to hide your thoughts from us, and we know and trust your judgment in all things that you do. So we have come to you for an accounting of your dealings with Tro-Ven and the manner of his death, for this may provide a clue for our unraveling. Upon such a flimsy thread hangs the life of Shar-Nuhn!"

Kla-Noh motioned his guest to a chair, then sat beside Si-Lun. "True it is that we were employed in the thwarting of Tro-Ven, and to his doom. But we were not unaided, for you may also know of the existence of his lovely and powerful daughter, whom he brought from another side of time into this world. That lord seems to have made a habit of injuring women and leaving them to their grief, for he wedded this lady's mother, who is now a queen, and plundered her of knowledge, love, esoteric arts, and finally their daughter. But the mother had taught her well, strengthening her spirit and her mind in the discipline of their knowledge. So, with some small aid from us, though it was principally good advice that we supplied, Li-Ah strove with her father, to such effect that he, his house, and all his servants were cast into the bay.

"Does it not seem, then, that in his ceaseless journeyings upon the earth and out of it, he may have encoun-

tered another such as Li-Ah's mother, and left her to grief
and anger? Few things, I have found, can evoke such
lasting and dangerous reactions in human beings as can
meddling with their children. So he did with the case we
know, begetting the child in full knowledge that his only
intention was to use her as his instrument, then wresting
her from her mother when he found such use for her.

"It well may be that another mother has been so
served, and that, cast into despair, she is avenging herself
upon all Shar-Nuhn, being unable to isolate him for pun-
ishment and all unknowing that he is dead. Does this
seem logical to you, Teacher of Men, or is it the dream-
spinning of an old man?"

"We are working with the stuff of dream—and of sorcery, Kla-Noh. For a hypothesis I came to you, and such
you have given me. Now have we need of those who can
seek out this desolate spirit, wrestle with her reason, per-
suade her that her enemy is beyond her reach, and bring
this torment to an end. Nu-Rea believes that the center of
the turbulence focuses upon the island of Ra-Mil, which
is upon the edge of the Far Islands, many days' journey
by ship, even in fair weather. Yet we have ways—the
Lord Tro-Ven, before he went astray after his own
strange and foolish goals, worked with us in producing
them—of sending persons about the world and into other
worlds by means of crystals of power." The Initiate
peered at the two Seekers from beneath his brows, his
pale eyes enigmatic.

"We will go, of course," said Si-Lun, reading Kla-Noh's
answer in his face.

"I am not so old and infirm that I cannot exert myself
in such a cause as this," said the Seeker, and his back
straightened, his color heightened, as he again smelled
the potent scent of action.

Ru-Anh smiled. "Such, I knew, would be your answer. And you two, who were involved in the fate of Tro-Ven, will carry more weight, I am certain, with yonder weatherwitch than any of us, trained though we may be in the ways of men. If you will but come to the Tower of Truth, as soon as may be, we will send you upon your way. And it may well be that the most dangerous span of your voyage will be that short one across the bay," he said, gazing, as Kla-Noh had done, slantwise through the louvers at the roaring waters.

"We are not grown so effete that it takes a great amount of packing up and readying," said Si-Lun. "Can you but wait for an hour, we will return with you to the Tower."

So it was that before the little light which the clouds admitted had left the sky the two Seekers and the Initiate had struggled through the wind to the craft that had brought Ru-Anh, and all were embarked upon the struggling backs of the waves. The prow thrust alternately skyward and into the depths as the cutter was tacked with consummate skill against the wind to reach the Tower.

In the lee of the Tower there was a small pond of calmer waters where they might disembark, but three dismally wet and draggled men made their way into the water entry beneath the stone steps that led to the great door.

Night was now come, and, upon consultation with the other Initiates, it was agreed that the Seekers would be well advised to rest the night before embarking upon their tenuous mission. So Kla-Noh and Si-Lun found themselves, some six hours after the knock upon their door, in a situation where they had never thought to be,

lying side by side in narrow cots in the room of an Initiate in the Tower of Truth.

Dawn found the Tower a busy hum of activity, as,
breakfasted and blessed, the two were ushered into a
chamber above the level of the Second Secret of Shar-
Nuhn. Much was there to arouse their interest, and many
questions they would have asked, had there been time.
But they were hurried into the alcove at the side of the
room, which was curved like the inside of a shell and
lined with ridged and polished crystal, bluer than a
dream of blue, with a translucence that hinted at depths
upon depths within. In the heart of the curve were fixed
two cushioned chairs, with light webbing to fasten about
the sitter. Here Kla-Noh and Si-Lun sat, after clasping for
a last time the hands of Ru-Anh and his acolyte Al-Tah.

When the fastenings were made firm, the two Initiates
moved into the chamber, where a curtain hid one wall.
The two Seekers could not see what they did there, but
the crystal began to glow with an internal flame, burning
deeper and deeper into its strange depths, and sparks of
white light began to flicker in its ridges.

Then the Seekers saw the chamber without pale into a
ghost, thinner and thinner, until it was gone as a mist on
the breeze. In its place, growing from a less-than-nothing
into an almost-something, appeared another chamber,
larger, and of a different shape. There, also, were two
robed figures, but their robes were of a dull golden mate-
rial, and their faces were unknown. When the new chamber was firm and fixed and real, the Initiates stepped into
their alcove and loosened the bonds of the two travelers.

"Greetings, Kla-Noh and Si-Lun," said the shorter of
the two, as he helped them to their feet and escorted
them forth from the alcove. "You will need food and a
short rest, for this mode of travel leaves one shaken and

ill at ease for some hours. Nonetheless, you will be restored and ready to go forward before the sun (were it visible at all) is overhead. We have a vessel provisioned and manned, for you still will have need for a half day's voyage to reach Ra-Mil, though a span of an hour would suffice if the winds and the waves were as usual."

Truly they were shaken, feeling as one does when rising from an illness, light in the bone and unsteady behind the eyes. But rest and food brought them to themselves, and they boarded their craft before noon and the two-man crew cast off. The storm seized them in its teeth and they struggled away, into the roil of wind and water.

Neither Kla-Noh, who had traveled much in his youth, nor Si-Lun, who was a sailor in other years, ever forgot that voyage. The ship groaned in the grip of the waves, and the tossing was such that the two Seekers needs must lash themselves to bunks below, so great was the risk of being lost overboard or of being dashed senseless below-decks.

Yet the prayers and the blessings of the Initiates bore fruit, for they moved through the wrack at a good speed and before night sighted the headland of Ra-Mil, all but obscured by the flying spume.

When they ran under the shelter of the island, moving under half-reefed topsails, and came into the anchorage, crew and passengers were alike amazed. For the island was as the eye of a hurricane. All was quietude, and no wind blew, though the storm circled about it in gray bitterness.

Thoughtfully the Seekers congratulated their two seamen and went ashore, where none came to greet the newcomers and no one was visible upon the streets of the small town that straggled down to the water's edge. Evening now being upon them, lights were visible behind high windows and through chinks, but no lights were lit in the streets, though torch standards hinted that such had been the custom.

Seeing a low house sporting a sign that portrayed a mermaid riding upon a dolphin, they hurried to it and entered. Inside was a room lit by sputtering lamps and half-warmed by a discouraged blaze upon the hearth. Along the sides of the room were long settles, which were occupied by a number of somber men with tankards in their hands. All looked up in something akin to alarm when Kla-Noh and Si-Lun entered.

The host, who had been sitting at a small table to the rear of the room with his round head upon his hand, looked around, then rose. "Enter, strangers, though you come upon an ill-omened wind," he said.

"Seldom have we seen men so glum," agreed Kla-Noh. "Would it have to do, my friend, with the strange weather that holds upon—and off—your pleasant island?"

The tavern keeper sighed and wiped his hands absently upon his apron. "Witch weather, witch weather it is, sirs, and no mistake. Not since yonder lady's grandmother's time has such come upon this land, and we know not how to deal with it."

"Know you the teachings of the Initiates?" asked Si-Lun.

"Aye, we do," answered the man, in a puzzled manner. "Now and again one of those kind people makes a home with us and teaches the young ones the ways of Truth. Surely we know the Initiates, though they are far off in times of sudden trouble, if none be quartered here then."

"We are sent by the Initiates of Shar-Nuhn, through those of the Far Islands, to inquire into this matter of weather and find a cure, if such may be done," said Kla-

Noh. "Can you tell us of this lady, and why she is blamed for the troubles of the sea and the sky?"

"In truth," answered the host, "if you are come from the Tower, you are welcome. Sit you down, and I will tell you of Lo-Sha, the weatherwitch, and her daughter and her granddaughter, who sits now upon the hill above us, shut into her round house, troubling the waters and the lands.

"When first our fathers came to this fertile island, it was inhabited by one very ancient family that had lived here from of old. This was when Lo-Sha, the weather-witch, was only a child, and none of her family spoke of her powers, which were growing with her, it seems to us now.

"The family welcomed the newcomers as neighbors and friends, and none knew enmity from any, until Lo-Sha became a woman. Such a woman was she that 'as beautiful as Lo-Sha' is still our term for a likely lass. Then, you may guess, trouble came, for three lads wished to marry her and none would she have. Being young and determined, they strove with one another and kept, one or another of them, under her feet until they came near to driving her mad.

"When her father saw how things were tending, he spoke with the families of the young men, warning them that his family were not as other people, that strange and violent powers were born in them, and that Lo-Sha was no spiritless and helpless maiden, to be forever pestered by suitors whom she did not desire. Then did the families attempt to discourage those youths from their course, but the spirit of competition, more than anything, I'd reckon, spurred them on.

"Then spoke Lo-Sha herself to each of them, saying, 'If you do not cease your pursuit and your frictions, I shall

howl up a wind to cool your ardors.' But they would not
listen, for how could one so slender and fair hope to
frighten great men such as they?

"Upon a day that dawned fair and bright, one of the
suitors made a final error. What it was none can say, but
it was the final fagot on the donkey-load for Lo-Sha. In
the midmorning, into the clear sky, there came a cloud
which my grandfather described to me so vividly that I
could see it myself. Black as a warlock's heart it was, and
full of wind, and it stooped upon this island and swept it
like a flail. One of the young men (yes, that one) was
blown clean away, and the other two frightened into per-
manent good behavior. In truth none had time for mis-
chief when it had done, for the houses were to reroof—or
to rebuild—and the haystacks were gone, the cattle scattered, the boats in the harbor stove in and their rigging
carried away.

"And from that time until now, none of us has inter-
fered with the family of Lo-Sha. She married, you must
know, one who came from another place, and not in any
craft we ever saw. He lived but a short time, but he left
her with a daughter, another such as she. And the daughter never had need to call down the winds, for we were
well warned. This daughter went away to Shar-Nuhn,
and there she married, bore a daughter, and died. Then
was her child brought back to Ra-Mil, and her grandmother brought her up, a lovely and modest maiden to
the eye, but with all the knowledge and power of her an-
cestors, we reckoned.

"Some winters agone, we learned that she, too, had
wed one who came by a way we cannot know. He was a
tall, arrogant fellow enough, who strode about looking
down his nose at our folk. Not long did he stay, but in the
early summer a daughter was born to Lo-Sha's grand-

daughter, Ril-Ah, and she brought the babe to the Initiate that she might bless it, and we all went up to see it. A proud lady she was, to be sure, and the babe a lovely one, fair and bright. Yet not six months since, the child's father returned, wanting to take her away, and her only a little toddling thing, needing her mother.

"In some places the law will hold with letting a father do what he likes with his own, but here we make our own law, and a child's rightful place is with its mother until it reaches an age of strength and wisdom enough to know its own mind. It was said"—and here the tavern keeper turned away his eyes—"that the great man was wild with anger when Ril-Ah denied him the little one. He stormed and he threatened, but little did she—or we—suspect that he would harm his own begotten daughter.

"Yet such he did. When he could not have her, he strangled that little one with his own hands, it looked to be, and left, however he came, I suppose, leaving Ril-Ah to find her child murdered and her murderer flown where she could not follow.

"For months she has sat in her house, alone, for her grandmother is dead, and none saw her come forth and no light ever shone at night, yet we know she lives, for we take food to the door and it disappears in the night. Then three days past, the storm arose that you can see, that does not touch us, but wreaks a wrath upon the world without. And we sit here, in fear and pity, unable to find what we should do or say, or even if we should do nothing."

Kla-Noh touched his hand gently. "You have done and said what is needful, my friend. We will do the rest. Serve ale all around for yourself and your friends, and direct us to the lady's house. When we return, there may be joy on your faces." And Kla-Noh laid a handful of coins upon the table and he and Si-Lun went to the door and took a lantern that their host pressed upon them, with directions.

They went away up the hill, a bobbing spot of light, which all in the tavern watched out of sight before turning to their ale.

The two Seekers went up to the round house that sat darkly upon the hilltop and rapped upon the low door. For a time no one came, but a dim light at last showed through the glass and a hand loosed the bolt.

When the door opened, they entered, courteously introducing themselves as they stepped across the threshold, and the door closed behind them. Then for a long time the house held only quiet conversation, though the light continued to shine behind the door. The low hum of the Seekers' voices was punctuated by the staccato of a higher tone, which seemed to ask many questions. At last the sounds died away into a taut stillness.

Then a change came in the air. The drone that was the offshore tempest began to die away, and far on the horizon a few feeble stars could be seen, struggling to twinkle. The airless, breathless tension of the island was loosened, and the men in the tavern below drew breath more easily and smiled at one another.

And when the door opened again, and the Seekers came forth, they were followed by a great cry: "May all the gods be praised! He is dead! He is dead!"

Then they went down the hill and boarded their vessel and sailed quietly away in the dawn light, on the turning tide.

VI

The Beast in the Barrens

The last of fall's honeyed days had been swept into night by the first of winter's bitter blows. The Purple Waters were battered by the sleet-laden winds, and the city of Shar-Nuhn huddled within its strong stone walls, well content to enter the semi-lethargy of its winter state.

In the house of Kla-Noh, Seeker After Secrets, and Si-Lun, his foster son, the fires leaped high in the shell-shaped hearths, and no breath of chill made its way through the tight walls and windows of their home to cool the old Seeker's bones. Seated before the fire in the sitting room, sipping spiced wine, the two made cheerful company, with their little servant. They had talked the evening to darkness and the darkness to bedtime, and now they sat lazily, dreading to move from their exceeding comfort. Each whimper of wind around the corners made their snugness more apparent and their good fortune more lovely.

Si-Lun spread his arms wide, stretching, and Kla-Noh stirred as if to arise, then stopped, frozen to stillness, as if listening.

"There is need," he said to Si-Lun. "Somewhere in this miserable night, there is one who has need of us two. Long have I lived on the edges of secret ways, and the silent voice of necessity can call me from afar. Make ready, with warm clothing and rough gear, for this night we go into the barrens to the west."

Si-Lun looked at him for the space of two heartbeats, his eyes lighting with understanding. "Make ready provisions such as will sustain us for some days," he said to Nu-Veh, the servant, "light to carry, with no need to cook, and put them, with spare clothing, into a large pack and a small one."

Without further words, the two Seekers hurried about changing into heavy tunics and trousers, warmly lined boots, and cloaks with fur mittens attached by thongs.

Before the cloud-hidden stars had moved two degrees across the heavens, the two were away, battling their way across the wind, moving steadily westward. Avoiding the outskirts of the city, they trudged along cart lanes and across stiff-stubbled fields, crunching the drifting sleet underfoot, feeling already the sting of the cold in their lungs.

The light of the seeing-glasses they carried did little save make the swirling ice visible, sparkling in bright flickers from the air and the earth. Now and again a lonely tree loomed before them, darkly as a wraith, or a bit of hedge or fence crossed their way. Yet even these grew fewer as they drew farther to the west, and before dawn they knew by the untrammeled beat of the wind that they had reached the barrens that girdled Shar-Nuhn upon the landward side.

Then they stood side by side and considered. "From this direction came the call," said Kla-Noh tiredly. "Yet I had thought that the last of those who sought to make their homes and pasture their herds here had abandoned the attempt long ago. Still comes the small cry that speaks to my spirit, and from the west. We must go on."

"My father-friend," said Si-Lun, "you are weary past walking, as am I. Rest we must, lest we fall and leave the cry unanswered forever. Let us shelter for an hour or two in the lee of the stones that rise ahead and then continue our journey in what light this storm will permit to reach from the heavens. When we have rested and eaten a little, then will we go forward more quickly."

So they rested, huddled against the stones, wrapped in their fur-lined cloaks, faces covered from the sting of the air. The pain of cold and age had entered into Kla-Noh's bones, and he shivered until Si-Lun opened his cloak and they huddled together, sharing their little warmth in the cold wastes.

But when the light came they were up and moving upon their way. Little comfort did it bring them to pause, so they moved doggedly toward the source of the call, which Kla-Noh now felt to be growing rapidly stronger. In midafternoon the wind abated and the sleet stopped. Soon thereafter they saw, far ahead, the stark and lonely silhouette of a house, and Kla-Noh knew it to be the source of the call that compelled him. Then did their weary feet hasten, and long before night they were at the door.

At their knock the heavy door was unbarred and unfastened from within, a process that took many minutes. When it swung open at last, a comely young woman stood in the light and beckoned them to enter.

"I knew that one had heard my prayer," she said. "I felt your coming, this night and day. None could I send for aid save my heart and my spirit, yet those were enough. Truly the gods hold the hands of those in need."

The room that the two entered was austere yet comfortable, with the small touches that speak of the hand of a loving woman. Upon the hearthrug sat three children, one a crawling babe. The fire was low, and the room was becoming chill, yet no wood was in the bin for replenishing the blaze.

The woman said, "For three days I have not moved past the door, and the store of fuel and food that my man left for me has run to nothing, use it grudgingly as I would. Days ago he should have returned from sheltering the cattle in the far ranges, yet he has not come. And I could not go out to the byre, the cold cellar, and the wood shelter, for there is a beast on the barrens which has been ramping at my door these days and nights. He has slain my dogs, or driven them away, for they cried lamentably, and I have heard their voices no more. Saw you nothing as you came into view?"

Si-Lun, tugging at Kla-Noh's boot, answered, "Nothing was visible of man or beast, but the light was not good, though the sleet no longer falls. No dogs did we see nor hear, nor their bodies."

Then Kla-Noh spoke, while he flexed his cold toes and rubbed his stiffened fingers. "We are Kla-Noh, who was a Seeker After Secrets, and Si-Lun, who seeks also. Yestereve, as we sat at ease before our hearthfire, I felt your call in my spirit, and we came with all speed. Seldom does it happen that one who is not of the same blood can hear the heart-cry of another, yet yours was clear and strong. Well it is that we have come, for soon your little ones would have been hungry and cold."

The young woman had looked attentively into the old man's face as he spoke. When he paused, she knelt before him and took his hands in hers. "Indeed the call of blood to blood is strong. Do you remember your uncle Ro-Van, the younger brother of your father? He was my grandfather, though I knew him little, for he was at sea until he reached a great age, and when he came ashore to stay, he soon died. Yet he spoke to my mother much of his family, and she to me. There was great pride among us that our kinsman was such an honored and able Seeker as Kla-Noh. That you have come in aid to your cousin but bears out our feeling for you. And I am Lo-Nah, daughter of Sa-Nel, daughter of Ro-Van, and your kinswoman."

The old man nodded thoughtfully. "It is true," he said. "Peace on your house, Lo-Nah. We will speak together while gathering your wood and provender, then we will rest the night, and tomorrow we shall go to seek your husband and to hunt the beast that has besieged you. Saw you this animal when it came?"

"Twice it came in the night, and there was no moon. I saw nothing, but we could hear its panting and grunting and scrabbling at the door. When it came again, it was day, but the storm had begun and nothing could be seen from the windows save the wind-whipped sleet. Yet I knew it to be near, for the dogs were ever growling and clawing at the door. At last I let them free, hoping that they could kill it or frighten it away, but I heard only their howls of fear and pain, and they never came to the door again. Whether it be bear or lion or monster from the barrens I cannot say," answered Lo-Nah.

"Then we must go cautiously," said Si-Lun, his eyes lighting with a fierce gleam. "Yet, with my long knife at my belt, I may hope to find and to slay this beast."

Before night the Seekers had made all well about the farmstead, replenishing the stores of food and fuel for Lo-Nah and her children. With darkness came the keening wind from the north and a light snow. Thankful were all within the house that they were sheltered from the bitter night, and long they talked before the dying coals of the fire.

At last all slept, Si-Lun and Kla-Noh rolled in heavy

rugs before the hearth. Still the snow fell without, and the pale drifts crept up the walls and slipped their chilly fingers into the crevices. Neither moon nor star could penetrate the clouds with light, but in the glimmer of snow light moved a shadow, humped and black against the pristine background.

Deep was the sleep of Kla-Noh, yet within the framework of his dream whispered a warning. With difficulty he drew himself from the depths and opened his eyes, seeking, by the faint glow of the coals, the forms of his companions. All were safely in place, and he lay wondering, listening, feeling within himself for the source of his unease. Then the night was split by an unhuman roar as a heavy body flung itself at the door of the house, thumping and scratching at it as if to bring it down.

At once Si-Lun was on his feet, flinging off the encumbering rug, his hand at his knife. Kla-Noh also rose, more slowly, and motioned to the woman to keep the children quiet, for they had wakened and were whimpering beneath their bedclothes.

"I shall go out the window at the back and take him from the side," whispered Si-Lun, reaching for his cloak.

"No," said Kla-Noh. "You are yet weary, and this is an unknown creature. Look from the window—you can see that snow is falling. The beast cannot get into the house and will soon return to its lair. By morning we shall have recovered our energies and will be at our best. Then we can trail it through the snow, taking it at our own time and choosing our own ground."

"But the snow may cover its track," protested Si-Lun.

"Should that be so, it will, I think, return here. We have but to wait. It is not the part of wisdom to attack the unknown in darkness, while we are yet stiff and bone-weary. Let us but reinforce the doorway with the chest beneath the window, then we shall sleep again."

This they did and returned to their places, though not to sleep for a long time, for the beast could be heard moving about the door, its heavy breathing loud in the quiet. Yet leave it did, at last, and the listeners sank into quiet slumber, undisturbed until morning.

With the first light, Si-Lun was examining the spoor left in the snow at the doorway. So light was the snow that, though it had fallen for long after the creature left the house, the hollows of its footsteps showed as bowl-shaped depressions, which led away westward. Yet did Si-Lun gaze upon them with a puzzled air, following their line to the edge of the house yard and back with inquiring eyes.

"No hunter I," he said to Kla-Noh, "yet I am not unfamiliar with beasts of many kinds. Their ways and their forms have been an interest to me since I was a lad in the mountains of the Far Continent. Yet this beast walks not upon four feet, I would say, but upon two. Still, its steps must shuffle, or its feet be large, for the hollows of its prints are long ovals, not roundish as would be the tracks of a man. Much interest have I in beholding this creature. Let us break our fast and be off."

Kla-Noh was also anxious to begin their quest, so their meal was quickly over and their farewells taken.

"We shall return with your man or with word of him," he said to Lo-Nah. "And should our tidings be of the worst, we shall bear you with us to Shar-Nuhn, to decide your future in the comfort of my home."

"My thanks to you, kinsman," wept Lo-Nah. "But I pray to the gods that you find Ka-Rod and return him to me, for my children need their father and I my husband."

Seeing the door firmly secured behind them, the two

Seekers went from the house yard out upon the barrens, where the wind worried at their cloaks and brought tears to their eyes. Undeterred, they followed the track, which led in a wavering manner still westward, over hummocks and around standing stones. In places there were spots where the thing had threshed about in the snow, as if in anguish, before moving again upon its way.

Occasionally the trail veered aside into a patch of scrub or standing grasses, and in such a place they found the body of a dog, stiff in the snow with a snarl upon its dead face. Its neck had been broken.

Then did Si-Lun and Kla-Noh look upon each other with a strange speculation in their eyes.

"Such is not the way of beast with beast," muttered the old Seeker, bending over the dog. "Such a break cries aloud of . . . hands. . . ."

Si-Lun grunted, squatting to peer along the ground. Then he rose and moved away from the trail, kicking aside the snow from a hummock that lay there. And there was the other dog, in like case with its companion. Then did Si-Lun look back along their track, toward the house of Lo-Nah.

"Much do I hope," he said, "that yonder lady will have no dreadful word upon our return."

Kla-Noh laid his hand upon the younger man's shoulder. "Do not despair, my friend. Should our suspicion be a reality, still there may be hope. Many ways are given by the gods to men in their extremity. Let us go on in hope and strength to find the truth of this mystery."

Then they went forward, following the track, until they sighted a hillock in the distance, crowned by a jumble of rock that had spilled down its side. There they left their path and circled to approach the place from the south, where they would have the cover of a gully

rimmed with snow-drifted thorn trees. By bending low,
they were able to come to the very edge of the hill without being discovered by whatever—or whoever—might be
hiding there.

As they reached the first of the stones, the wind died
entirely away, leaving that strange snow silence which
seems to press upon the ears. Instinctively they paused to
listen. No sound seemed abroad in all the expanse of the
lands about them. Si-Lun shifted his pack and lifted his
foot to step forward. But he froze in the midst of the
movement, for a racking moan sounded from the hillock.
Not quite like the moan of a man was that sound, yet
unlike the mindless cries of an animal. A sound of anguish, as of a beast that had just realized its beasthood,
moved across the cold air to the Seekers, who stood,
heads bowed and hands clenched, until it died away.

Kla-Noh unstrapped his pack and laid it in the snow,
gesturing to Si-Lun to do likewise. He fumbled with mit-
tened hands in its depths for a moment, bringing out a
packet, which he placed beneath his cloak. Then the two
moved into the rocks.

So still was the day, that quiet sound they followed
seemed loud, and it was the work of few moments to
track it to its source. In a dark cranny among the rocks,
huddled in a deep corner, they saw the creature they
sought. It lay with its head to the wall, its feet drawn up,
and it keened wearily, hopelessly. And it was a man.

Kla-Noh's rutted face seemed made of stone as he said,
"It must be the husband of Lo-Nah. The Initiates have
told me, long years agone, that these barrens were forbid-
den to our kind for cause. Though there be fertile places
where the grass grows tall, soil that would turn sweetly to
the plow, yet there are also places where a deadly
sickness oozes from the very rock and moves in the air.

Such ills are these as are not known among the haunts of men, turning sufferers into beasts, little by little, as their minds leach away. Much did I fear, when Lo-Nah told us of her husband's absence, that the beast she so feared was he whom she longed to see.

"Yet it was not truly he. Enough of himself remained to send him blindly homeward, as any hurt beast goes to his lair. But had she seen, when he came, and opened the door—I shudder when I think what might have happened."

Si-Lun had listened in stillness, but now he said, "Yet you said to me that we must go on in hope, and that the gods lend aid to those in need. Was the hope to be only that what you feared might not be? And can even the gods restore one so stricken?"

His father-friend took from his cloak the packet and unrolled the silken binding. Within was a crystal of more than topaz richness of color. Palm-sized it was, flat on the one side and cut into gemlike facets upon the other. Within its amber-golden heart there seemed a flame of life, a pulse of power that glowed outward, even into the snow brightness of the day.

Before entering the cleft of rock, Kla-Noh placed the crystal upon his bared hand and, for a moment, laid the other hand upon it, warming it between them. Then he stooped and went in to the unfortunate being within, and Si-Lun followed, wondering, doubting, yet with hope awakening within his heart.

Kla-Noh bent over the man, who, sensing his presence, tried to lunge upright. Si-Lun was there, however, and held him fast, pinning him to the ground with his weight and strength, yet he was forced to struggle mightily.

"Hold him so for one instant," hissed Kla-Noh, "and I will calm him."

Then he cupped the glowing crystal in his palm and laid his hand upon the sufferer's brow, holding the gem to his forehead. At once the struggling ceased, and the poor creature lay moaning quietly, with his eyes focused upon something deep inside himself.

Kla-Noh bent above him again and turned the crystal with its facets upward. Then he reached out his hand to Si-Lun, who gripped it silently, slipping into a crouch against the rocky wall. The old man gazed then deeply, deeply into the heart of the crystal, and when his eyes were fully focused upon it, it glowed still brighter, until it seemed a small sun set upon the brow of the ragged and helpless man.

From the air above the gem there came a whisper that grew in strength as time passed. Si-Lun felt, as the glow waxed and the whisper strengthened, his vitality flowing out, through his hand, through his companion, into that brilliant stone.

"We are here. We are here. We are here," whispered the stone.

"There is need," said Kla-Noh, speaking into the gem. "Send your seeking thought into the western barrens. Think upon Kla-Noh and Si-Lun, whom you know. Look through our eyes and through this crystal Shamal, which you gave to me. Regard this one who has passed through the poisoned places."

Then Si-Lun felt, for the first time, the touch within his mind that was the presence of an Initiate, which looked through him as though he were the far-seeing glass he used to use in his seafaring days. An awesome thing it was, yet not frightening. He stood aside, within his soul, and let another peer through his senses.

"And is this one worthy of the great effort you seek?" whispered the voice in the air.

"Him I know not," answered Kla-Noh. "But he is the man of my kinswoman, and has been a true and faithful husband to her and a kindly father to his children. Even in his agony he sought to return to his own, though he was more than half a beast. Look within him. We will give you all of our strength of body and spirit. Look deeply into his trapped self, crying within its beast prison."

And then there was a surge of power through the two Seekers that was physical agony for both. The strength ran from their bodies like water, and light moved through their minds and seemed to leap from their eyes. They felt the Initiates within them seeking the truth within the man between them, and they clasped their hands together, and Kla-Noh held the jewel as if it were their anchor to the world of life.

Then the awful force slackened, and the whisper came again. "He is worthy of the task. Hold you to your spirits' foundations, and we shall join our strengths to yours, to work the cure of this rash but honest man."

Hardly was there time for a deep-drawn breath, for a closing of burning lids over drying eyes, for a gasp of "Hold fast" through dried lips.

Then they felt themselves seized in a mounting wave of potency. Inside their souls they could feel the presence of many, men and women of virtue beyond that of normal humankind, all united in a terrible effort, all striving together against a blind and mindless darkness. Through the jewel poured the flood of power, into the clouded brain of the man upon the cave floor.

The two Seekers sat hunched, enduring the unendurable flood of force, linked inseparably to the forged chain that they anchored. The man's eyes turned outward, slowly, slowly, and his breathing ceased to rasp in his

throat and his muscles eased. Still the power flowed into
the fogged mind, which now grew ever clearer.

Ka-Rod looked out through his own eyes and spoke
with his own voice. "I am again a man," he said wonder-
ingly. "No more a beast on the barrens, homeless and desolate. You have made me a man again. The gods have not
yet left us to the awful play of chance." Then he wept,
and when the tears flowed, the power dwindled and died.

The voice from the gem said, exhaustedly, "It is well.
We have wrought in the names of the gods this day to
bring this man back from the outer blackness. Our
brother Kla-Noh and our brother Si-Lun, you have
wrought as none save those of our order have ever
wrought before. Henceforth you are linked with us in
brotherhood. Go in peace."

The glow died from the crystal, and Kla-Noh lifted it
in a hand that trembled with weariness and wrapped it
and put it again within his cloak. Si-Lun loosed his clasp
upon his friend's hand, and it was difficult, so cramped
were their muscles with their long striving. The two
rested for a while against the cave walls. Then they made
a little fire from thorn branches and warmed the weak
Ka-Rod. From their retrieved packs they brought food,
and all ate, comforted by the light of reason that shone
from Ka-Rod's eyes.

Night was now upon them, and they gathered a store
of thorn branches and rested away the hours of darkness,
tending their patient, who gained strength every hour.
When light touched the east, Ka-Rod said, "Now I am
able to move from this place. Take me home to my people, that their long wait may be ended." And he took
their hands and stood erect, as a man. "Yet how may I
say to my dear ones that I have been a beast?"

"For the comfort of your wife," said Kla-Noh, "say only that we found you overcome with sickness."

Then the three moved away over the snow, toward the east and Lo-Nah, and never did she know what had been the beast at her door.

VII

The Flaming Feather

Kla-Noh stood upon his terrace, looking across the amethyst that touched the Purple Waters. The evening meal was set within his chamber, and Si-Lun stood at the door, but still the old man lingered in the afterglow, as if waiting.

Above him, in the cupola that housed his dovecote, the murmur of pigeon voices soothed the soft air, and he looked up with a smile. His eyes widened then, and he gestured upward, that Si-Lun, too, might see.

From the zenith, it seemed, came a dark dot, circling downward in spiral swoops toward the pigeon loft. As it veered over the Bay of Shar-Nuhn, the light caught its snowy feathers, gilding it to a shape of flame. And as it spread its wings to glide into the loft, both of the men could see that its breast was touched with scarlet that came from no trick of light.

"My friend," said Kla-Noh, "that is no bird of mine. Nor is it one that has visited my loft before. Yet I felt a coming that I no longer feel, so this small one must be a messenger. Let us go up into the dovecote."

Then Si-Lun took the old man's arm, and they went in and up. But when they stood in the loft and Kla-Noh took the bird in his gentle hand, there was no quill fixed to its leg, no written message anywhere about its body.

Then a smile again lit the face of the old Seeker, and it was mirrored in the face of his friend and helper, for such a riddle was the joy of their beings and the delight of their thoughts. For many weeks they had pursued their studies and their pastimes, but the sameness of the days had begun to pall, and the need for action was upon them.

Carefully they turned the bird about, examining him closely. Pure white he was, with feet and beak of a clear ruby hue. His eyes were bright and looked upon his handlers without fear—even with something like understanding. Upon his breast there blossomed one feather of burning scarlet.

"This is no bird bred in Shar-Nuhn," said Kla-Noh at last. "Nor is he of any breed that I know, for none that I have ever seen bears that ruby color. As for the feather above his heart, that is no inborn trait of his. It has been dyed, and by a wavering hand. This, my son-in-heart, is a cry for aid, or I am no Seeker. What think you?"

"Of birds I am no judge," answered Si-Lun. "But of secrets I am an old riddler. No doubt is there in my heart. This is a message sent by one who, for unknown reasons, can send no other."

Kla-Noh set the pigeon in a nest hole and closed the netting that covered its entrance. Through a small opening in the top he dropped grain, and a soft "tack! tack!" began, as the pigeon ate.

Then the two went down to their own supper, and long they talked over the wine cups after Nu-Veh had cleared away their plates. Speculation was interesting but fruitless, for the imagination had all the points of the compass through which to move.

At last the old Seeker set down his empty cup and ran his finger meditatively about its rim. "We have no direction," he mused, "in which to guess. But one there is who knows the proper course, and that is our small guest. Something there is in his eye that speaks of purpose. The map of his journey is imprinted upon his spirit, and he will retrace his flight when we set him free."

"Though we cannot fly after him, we can note the exact direction of his flight," said Si-Lun. "And for what reason do we maintain a stout vessel if not to travel in her? If the bird is indeed sent to bring aid, then it will be likely to speed directly home from our loft. Why do we not take a like course and follow as the wind wills, keeping our eyes sharp for any untoward sign?"

His foster father laid his hand upon the young man's wrist. "My thought has moved with yours, and a little ahead," he said. Then he called, "Nu-Veh!"

The little servant trundled his round shape into the chamber and bowed. "Yes, my master?"

"We are like to take a longish journey, my friend. Look to the provisioning of our vessel. Then you may take yourself to your rest."

The small man bowed again, then looked up with a wistful expression upon his moon face. "Never, O wise Kla-Noh, have I gone journeying with you. Many times I have made the packs or provisioned the craft for your adventuring, but never have I partaken of the joys of travel. Might I not go, this one time, to taste what adventure may be?"

The old Seeker looked with some surprise upon Nu-Veh. "Indeed, often we would have joyed in your company, but I have thought of your family's need for you and have never asked that you part from them for such indefinite spans of time as our journeys may be. Yet if you truly wish to come, this you may do. Our house shall be shut up, and we will name one to care for your wife and younglings until our return. Does this please you?"

But he did not need to ask, for the little man's face was crinkled into a grin of delight. He made no answer but bowed again and hurried away to make all ready for his great adventure.

Then Kla-Noh turned to his companion. "I feel the shaping hands of the gods at work, Si-Lun. No hint had our servant given of a desire to go wandering, before now. Some part he has to play in that which is to come, as have we, who follow on the path of a bird in flight. Let us make ready the craft; then we must go to our own rest, for the tide turns soon after sunrise, and we must be ready to follow our guide."

Morning flamed across the Purple Waters in bands of rose and gold and the edge of the sky was crossed with plum-colored cloud when the Seekers loosed the pigeon from the loft and watched him wheel upward, then arrow northward and east, in a direction that held no lands upon the maps of Shar-Nuhn. Yet the Seekers consulted their lodestone and charts and laid out a course to match.

Their sails unfurled and caught the wind like sun-colored petals, and the little craft that bore them danced away, out of the bay, into the rush of the Purple Waters. The hearts of the Seekers were bubbles of joy, and that of Nu-Veh was warm with delight, for the breeze bore them truly upon their course, and the feel of the day promised weather to come, that being the only spice of danger that had been lacking. They sped down the wind in a flurry of spray, and greenlings leaped before the bow as if in an excess of spirits.

Night found them still upon their course, though with lessened sail for caution's sake. There being three, two

could sleep while one tended the steering, and there was
no need to heave to in the hours of darkness. And it was
very dark. The moon that should have been near full and
that which should have been a rim of light near the horizon were obscured by racks of cloud that fled northward,
impelled by winds which had not yet descended to the
surface of the sea.

The dawn of the second day was direly different from
the first. For the winds had found the lower ways, and
the waters were lashed into towering waves that pitched
the small vessel first high and then low, and if she had
not been a stable and seaworthy craft in the hands of a
master seaman she might have been dismasted or even
lost. But Si-Lun held the tiller, and his hands and eyes
and heart worked together in the harmony of the gods.
So they rode out the storm, which had borne them many
leagues upon their way in a time shorter than they had
dreamed was possible.

The Seekers, old seafarers that they were, thought little
of the storm, for the Purple Waters held such surprises
for travelers upon their ways. But poor Nu-Veh had gone
no farther upon the sea than the confines of the Bay of
Shar-Nuhn, and his inward self was sorely ill. While Si-
Lun tended the steering, Kla-Noh held a basin for his little servant and spoke kind words to him and reassured
him in every way that he could find. Yet it was only with
the calming of the storm that the little man rallied and
decided that he would not die, perhaps.

That calming came with nightfall of their third day at
sea, and Nu-Veh was not alone in his thanksgiving. That
night they hove to, steadied by a sea anchor, and all slept
deeply and long. And when the sun rose, trailing bands of
warm-colored cloud about its disk, it showed upon the uttermost horizon a speck—a mere hint—that might be land.

With all speed the three cleaned the storm's traces from themselves, ate their breakfasts, and bundled in the sea anchor. Then, sails hoisted to catch the faint breath of air that stirred aloft, they made for that speck in the distance.

As they neared, they could see that something glinted in the sunrise, even before they could discern the shape of the land. Then they could see that they approached a steeply pitched island that rose sharply from the sea's edge to a wooded crest. Upon that crest shone a round-topped building, not large, but shining white and gold in the newly minted sunlight. Something about that building filled them with delight. Its shape satisfied the eye, its color was pristine, its setting was perfection. Yet that could not explain the joy they felt at the sight of it.

They drew closer yet, and they could see, wheeling in exultant clouds about the dome, a storm of white pigeons whose flickering wings caught the light in shifting sparks. And as the Seekers anchored in the small cove that served as shelter, they could hear the many-feathered whisper of wings moving in the air.

Kla-Noh looked up and raised his hands in exaltation. "Many fair things have I seen in my long years," he said, "but none so glorious as this."

Then they walked up a winding path among noble pines that added their murmur to the whispering of wings, beneath a canopy of soaring shapes that dipped and whirled, coming low to study them with ruby eyes, then gliding away, higher and higher, toward the snowy pile at the summit. So they came out of the shadow into a purity of white light that shook their hearts with its wonder. Upon white pavement patterned with dim mosaics of blue they stood, washed in glory.

For many heartbeats they remained motionless, drink-

ing in the perfection of the place. Then Kla-Noh took one
step and said, "This is the place we sought. I feel it in the
deeps of my spirit. Here have the gods brought us, not to
gawk but to do their work. Let us find the door."

Then his companions woke from their ecstasy and
joined him in his search. Around the building they went,
marveling at the pierced-stone lace that screened its narrow windows, at the delicate buttresses that braced its
many-angled walls. Upon the other side, deep-hidden in
blue shadow, was the door. And at sight of it they
stopped in astonishment, for it was narrow and low,
hardly of a size to accommodate a full-grown man, even
should he bend and sidle. It was of wood, worn and
weathered so deeply that the inscription which they
could see had been cut into it was no longer legible.

It was a humble and a humbling door, a reminder to
any of humankind that their place in the scheme of the
gods was small indeed. Kla-Noh studied it for a long
while, then he reached a tentative finger and touched its
upper panel, and the door swung open.

Inside, there was deep blue silence.

Si-Lun put out his hand and touched the wall to steady
himself, for he felt as if he were falling forward into a
cool well or up into a strange sky, or out of himself entirely. Kla-Noh, who had known many secret things of
the gods, was less moved, but his spirit sang inside him,
as it did when he moved in holy places. Nu-Veh, awed to
his core, backed from the door and retreated into the
light. Under the cloud of pigeons he awaited his fate, for
he could not force himself to move into that tower of silence.

But the two Seekers went forward, as if into their own
home, confident and purposeful. Their footfalls sank into
the well of quiet and disappeared, and their breath made

no sound upon the still air. But their eyes glowed and their lips were curved into smiles and their steps were sure upon the midnight tiles of the floor and the dark marble of the stair that curved away upward in a tight spiral.

Before they reached the top of the stair, they found a silver cord hanging down the open core of the stairway. Kla-Noh tugged at it, without result, then tugged harder. An infinitely wistful chiming filled the air, as though a hundred bells, toned from deep-throated contralto to delicate treble, had been set in motion. As the magical notes fell about them, a door at the top of the stair opened, and a shaft of light severed the darkness.

A voice, so frail and thin that it spun down through the tower as tenuously as a cobweb, came through the door above them. "Well met," it whispered. "Come to me. . . ."

They hurried, then, up the stair and through the door. The room they entered swam in silver light from the sky and the sea. Ripples of glowing light quivered across the curving walls and danced upon the ceiling. A faint scent of herbs filled the air, and the Seekers felt a sense of freshness and fitness as they entered the glimmering chamber.

The man who lay upon the couch in the center of the room seemed neither fresh nor fit; his blue robe hung about his frame, showing its gauntness, and his transparent hands rose from his breast in supplication. The face that turned toward them was framed in soft white beard, but the eyes that seemed to seek for them looked where they were not, and they knew that the old man was blind.

Kla-Noh moved to kneel beside the couch. He caught the groping hands and guided them to his face.

"We have come, friend, in the wake of your pigeon and with the help of the gods, to aid you," the Seeker said. "How came you in these straits, without one to help you?"

The ancient took the Seeker's hand in his and, after great effort, sat upright. He turned his sightless eyes toward Kla-Noh and said, "I am Menelil, servant of the gods and watcher of the stars. Alone I dwell upon this island, which is known to few save those of my brothers and sisters in the Towers of Truth of the northern lands. For many tens of years I watched the stars from the top of this tower, noting their motions and calculating the orbits of the planets. For company I had my pigeons, which were as my own children, and when I was lonely or ill I made communication with my people through an instrument that we use.

"No fear had I of being left helpless. Yet the use of the Shamal requires eyes, and I woke, a week ago, without the power of sight. Then I knew that I must seek aid in another way, and I called at my window until a bird flew to my hand. No message could I write, but I trusted in the gods and set a sign upon its breast. I have waited in faith, but my food has long since been used, and I cannot find the strength to struggle in darkness seeking more.

"And you have come, as I knew the gods would contrive."

Then Menelil lay back upon his pillow and closed his eyes. Kla-Noh looked to Si-Lun, but that young man had gone to set Nu-Veh to cooking bland dishes to nourish their host. The old Seeker smiled and looked about after the Shamal of his host, for he knew that he was versed in its use and might thereby summon those who would care for the old man.

But though a soft leather bag lay upon the table beside

silken wrappings of a size to hold the Shamal, no topaz jewel could he find. He woke Menelil from his sleep to ask, and the ancient gestured toward the table.

"I took it from its swathings, trying if I might waken its power by the warmth of my hands alone," he said. "I left it upon the table. Is it not there?"

Kla-Noh searched again, though the table was bare save of the wrappings, and the floor beneath was innocent of any trace of the Shamal. "No," said he. "It is gone."

Then the old man laid his hand to his brow and said, "I tamed a corax that often ate among the pigeons. Its great black shape amused me, and the quickness of its mind was a pleasure. Often it would fly in at my window to visit me in my chamber. It loved to pick at any bright object—once it pilfered a lens from my instrument. It may be that the Shamal tempted it."

Kla-Noh nodded to himself. "Aye, that is likely. But it will sadly delay the bringing of your people to your side. We must return to our own Initiates, that they may give word to yours. And, in my unpardonable haste, I came away without my own Shamal."

A step was heard at the door, and Si-Lun entered bearing a steaming bowl whose fragrance brought Menelil upright upon his couch. The young man, his green eyes concerned, knelt beside the elder and held the bowl, guiding the trembling hand that wielded the spoon. When he was done, Menelil lay back and sighed, "Long has my order taught that none should think overmuch of his food, to the detriment of his spirit. Yet never have I known anything so comforting as that soup. May the man who cooked it be long blessed."

A timid voice at the door said, "My thanks to you, Lord, for your blessing," and the round face of Nu-Veh peered around the doorframe. "If I go adventuring," he said to Kla-Noh, "it ill becomes me to skulk in the sunlight while my master ventures into fear. Yet now that I am here, I find that this is a place of joy, and not of fear at all. And yonder Lord will need my art of cookery for many a long day to come."

Si-Lun raised his eyes to Kla-Noh, and the older man inclined his head. Understanding and wonder passed between them. Then Kla-Noh took the hand of the old Initiate in his own and said, "Friend Menelil, as we who are Seekers and seamen will be needed upon the return journey, we shall leave with you our friend and servant, Nu-Veh, who is a man of quiet and good sense, experienced at nursing the sick, and a cook of no mean skill.

"Never had he shown a desire to attend us upon our ways until now, but so cunning is the working of the gods that they placed the thought in his heart, and here he is where he is most needed. And when your people come to you, they will send him home to us and to his folk."

Thus it was that the craft that had come with three returned bearing only two. As they turned from the island, the Seekers looked back to wave to Nu-Veh, whose round figure stood solidly upon the terrace at the top of the hill. About him swirled and swung the rustling throng of pigeons, glinting white and gold in the late morning sunlight. From the tower window, high above beneath the dome, a pale hand fluttered, and they lifted their own arms in salute to Menelil.

Then they set their backs to the land and sped toward Shar-Nuhn.

VIII

The Eaters of Hearts

Low swung the sun, and the shadows of sails stretched long on the Purple Waters. The prow of the vessel dipped smoothly from wave to wave as the steady breeze pushed her homeward toward Shar-Nuhn.

The tiller was lashed, so even was the wind and so gentle the weather, and Si-Lun lay at his ease upon the deck, keeping an occasional eye upon the progress of the voyage. Kla-Noh had settled his older bones upon a coil of rope and leaned against the mast, watching the seas as they swelled past the speeding ship.

"Once before," mused Kla-Noh, "had I such a silken-smooth journey. Long ago it was, when I was heart-whole and carefree and never thought to spend my days as a Seeker After Secrets. We sped then east instead of west, away from Shar-Nuhn for the first time in all my life, and I was agog with excitement. But I am maundering, which is the cardinal sin of age. Sing us a song, Si-Lun, and I will be silent."

"No song shall I sing," answered his foster son, "until I have heard the tale of your first voyage. Seldom do you speak of your youth, and when you do, I am determined to hear."

So Kla-Noh settled himself more comfortably upon his

coil and, gazing into the indeterminate line that divided sea from sky, he told this tale.

* * *

My father was a merchant. Not a great merchant lord as was our late acquaintance, but well enough to do in a small way. His brother captained a vessel that traded afar, going past the Far Islands into the wild waters that wash the continent of your birth, and farther still. He alone, among all the captains of Shar-Nuhn, had dared the storm-ripped straits to circle about that land and to find the unknown islands and oceans that he knew must be upon the other side.

He returned from that first voyage into the farthest waters with a cargo of strange wares that made a fortune for his ship's owners and another smaller fortune for himself and my father. For his sharing of the cargo he took in goods and entrusted them to my father to turn them into gold.

There were fabrics in that cargo that set the women wild, so smooth were they, yet with intricate colored patterns woven into their texture with great art. There were items of wrought metal, both for use and for pleasure, that rivaled any our rulers had ever owned, yet they had been traded cheaply to my uncle in return for spices and heavy tools and other goods that are ordinary among us.

The lords who owned the ship were set afire with desire for more rich voyages, so they called my uncle, Ro-Van, to them and set him another such task. When I heard that he was to return to those shining, untouched shores, I besieged my father with such importunate words that he consented that I might go in the *Sar-La* with my uncle. With me he sent some store of gold for purchase of goods for his business, that he might show a

profit even upon such a pleasure voyage as mine would
likely be. And right willingly I accepted his commission,
fancying myself as a great trader, even a merchant lord,
perhaps.

So, upon a day that was pale and clear as sun through
ice, we hoisted anchor and sailed out of our old, familiar
bay, into the full wash of the Purple Waters, running before a fair wind with all our canvas spread to make full
speed.

Seeing that I was more than likely to hamper the working of the crew, my uncle made me a lookout and set me
high in the mast basket, bidding me watch for land, or
whales, or dark clouds upon the horizon. I soon realized
his purpose, but such was my delight in my exalted post
that I gave no indication that I knew he was only ridding
the deck of me. Swinging dizzily at the masthead, I
gloried in the limitless sky about me and the rolling purple seas that creamed at the bow. I had a fine head for
heights, and I spent long hours sprawled in the basket,
watching the little ship below me swing to left and to
right, fore and aft, feeling myself a fixed point between
sky and sea. Perhaps my uncle had likewise loved that
place in his days as a common seaman, for he made it my
daily duty, and I sat in the sky and dreamed away many
days of that enchanted voyage.

The Far Islands were our first landfall, for we took the
windward route, avoiding the longer, traveled routes of
short-haul traders. Never before had I heard our tongue
spoken with an alien twist to the sound, or seen the odd
ways in which other peoples clothe themselves. I was
aship and ashore by turns, trying to see all that was to be
seen in the short while it took to renew our water casks
and provisions. From the little store of gold that was my
own, I purchased for myself a small monkey from a boy

who stood upon the wharf, for I found its sad eyes and its little-old-man expression too tempting to resist.

Then the gong was rung upon the afterdeck, and the crew came running from their tasks ashore, and the lines were cast off. Once again we moved before the wind, clearing the fair harbor and dipping our flag as we rounded the crag that guarded the bay.

Away we flew again, with such a wind as a sailor dreams of at our backs and our faces turning ever toward the northeast. High in my basket, I gazed until my eyes ached, hoping to see the far bulk of the continent which we would soon raise, but to my great disappointment it rose from the sea in the night and was a well-defined line of darkness against the dawn light.

Seabirds yammered about my perch, and the distant resinous scent of forests came down the wind. I yearned toward the land, dreaming of the strange cities and peoples it might hold, but our destination lay not in that direction, and my uncle changed his course slightly, to run coastwise, keeping ample sea room, should the wind grow to a gale. For weeks we kept company with that distant shore, seeing, from time to time, huge logs of timber that had doubtless been borne down some river from the mountains to the sea.

Fish there were in plenty, great schools of them at times, accompanied by a canopy of screaming birds. Those who were not needed for working the ship were set to catching them and salting them down, against our passage of the straits, for my uncle was a thrifty manager and saved his masters' gold, gave his men a treat, and assured us of ample supplies, all in one. Catching the long, striped greenlings was a joy, for they fought the line and tossed at the hook, many succeeding in escaping thus. But I was not so happy when set to cleaning them and salting down the long strips, to be dried in the sun on the hatch covers. Ro-Van was firm. "None shall say that I cosset my brother's son. You are no child to loll in the shade while other men work. If you wish to eat of our catch, when need is upon us, then you must help to secure it."

So I cleaned fish and salted fish, until I smelled from end to end as if I were a fish myself. But when we were finished, then all hands stripped and washed in bucket after bucket of stinging cold water from the sea. Then I would climb again to the masthead and let the wind drive the stink from my nostrils as I rocked there with Mip, my monkey, clinging to my neck or the iron rim of the basket.

Thus we sailed, bearing ever north by east, until the coastline of the continent began to fall away eastward. Then my uncle changed course and steered due east, drawing near the towering crags that lined the mountainous shore. Then we began to see the handiwork of men, for there were inlets where fishing boats berthed, with sheds and wharves that spoke of preserving and drying and seaward trade.

As we made our way eastward, the mountains lessened in size and farmsteads became numerous, and soon we were hailed by a strangely rigged vessel that cut across our bows in the manner of officials in every land and time. And indeed they carried pilots and permits, both of which we should need in entering the great seaport which was now near, though hidden by a headland.

If I had been agog before, now I was speechless, for the harbor into which we put was overflowing with traffic, and the city was a greater city than two Shar-Nuhns rolled into one. No great-winged sea vessels were there, but many and many trawlers and fishermen and coastwise traders, together with long, narrow ships with tall triangular sails made of many-colored strips of canvas. My uncle said that those were from the farther oceans, whither we were bound.

I all but forgot the dignity befitting my nineteen years in staring and listening and smelling and feeling all that was to be sensed in that port. The language we knew was seldom to be heard there. Tongues of every cadence lilted in the broad avenues leading to the docks, and raiment of every shape and hue dazzled my eyes. While my uncle dickered for provender, with much waggling of hands and marking in the dust of the dockside, I roamed as far as I could go without losing sight of the masts of the *Sar-La*.

When the gong sounded, I was soon aboard, clinging to Mip with one hand and to my varied purchases with the other. But when once more we rode the wind, free upon the waters, I turned and looked with regret upon that wonderful city, wishing that there had been time enough for seeing all therein.

Now we made for the straits that were the sole passage between our Purple Waters and the seas beyond. Some days passed, and the weather grew less warm, less easy, but our following wind held. A day out from the narrows, we began to spy huge crags of rock thrusting into the upper air from the deeps. Then we reefed sail and went cautiously, with an old seaman upon my masthead, armed with a glass for sighting shoal waters and submerged rocks.

Now our faithful wind veered fitfully, gusting from north and west and south, raising gobbets of spume from the wave tops. Pinnacles of rock closed in, boxing us into the treacherous passage, where teeth of sharp stone grimaced at our frail keel as we edged this way and that, seeking clear passage. Just as we stood well into the cleft, the wind howled into a gale, flinging us helplessly among the waiting obstacles. Being unable to aid in the battle, I lashed myself to the mast and watched in awestricken wonder as my uncle, taking the wheel himself, shouted orders into the wind, sent seamen aloft to reef what sail was yet spread, and saw with eyes above and below, to right and left, every threat to his vessel.

More than once came the scraping and grinding of stone on keel, but always he sheered away before she was holed. How he saw the passage I cannot tell, for the wind-whipped spray obscured the air and dimmed the eyes. No seaman could remain in the mast basket, nor could he have seen our way from there. Yet my uncle, with the eyes of his spirit, held his ship in his hands, together with all our lives, and for a space of hours steered us through that dreadful strait.

When the *Sar-La* once again felt open sea beneath her, she sprang forward into the new-fallen darkness, until Ro-Van judged her to be well clear of the rocks and the shoals of the strait. Then we rode easily under staysails, with only the steersman on watch, while all rested from the ordeal. And the wind, as if regretting her treachery, followed fair as before.

When morning dawned, I was aloft with the light, gazing with delight at the sun trail that danced across waters which were a dazzling blue. Still we held our eastering, into the eye of the sun, and a cloud of white seabirds haunted our wake. With Mip on my shoulder, I reveled in the beauty until a growl in my middle reminded me of my uneaten breakfast.

My uncle sat in his cabin, eating his meal in good spirits. When I sat and spoke, he smiled at me as brightly as had the sunrise, and I was glad with him.

"Never, my uncle, have I seen a man guided by the

gods, until now. The Initiates have told me that such was possible, but I, being unwise in the world's ways, thought this to be a tale for children. Yet now I know it to be true."

"May you be so guided at need," said Ro-Van. "A clean mind and an honest heart and concern for your duty and your fellows must be yours, else no aid will come, never forget. And once the gods have moved your hands and looked out through your eyes, never again will you be tempted from the ways of rightness."

I turned this in my mind as I ate. Many of my fellows in Shar-Nuhn had boasted of exploits of doubtful honesty and no virtue, and I had been envious of their carefree devilry. Yet now I was glad that my bent for loneliness and thought had kept me free of such limiting deeds. I felt that even I might find the help of the gods if I but kept to the teachings of the Initiates and enjoyed the good of life without dabbling into the wells of darkness.

Then, with the inconsequence of youth, I fell to wondering how many days' voyage would see us approaching the lands that my uncle had visited before.

But my uncle, when asked, only chuckled and said, "Much we must do, mending rigging and ripped canvas, painting our scraped keel, scrubbing down and polishing up, before we sight A-Lakis, which is the first of the Farthest Islands. Do not fret, Kla-Noh, my nephew. You will find yourself there before you think to."

Truth was in his words. All was a bustle aboard the *Sar-La* for days as she scudded through those azure waters. When the darkness fell, and a round moon laid her path across the ebony wave tops, we were too weary to sit and dream, but fell into sleep at once.

Yet work as we did, before the damage of passage was all smoothed away the round-topped cloud that marked

an island was sighted, and before night we hove to, in
order to enter the unfamiliar harbor in full light. That
night, indeed, I dreamed. But morning brought the reality, and Mip and I were well forward (our post in the
basket being entrusted to a more experienced seaman
than I) when my uncle had canvas loosed again upon the
breeze.

The harbor was well protected by reefs and rock, and
it was set in an island far larger than any I had expected.
No great wharf was there, but many small jetties ran into
the water, and sailboats and rowing craft and fishing vessels lined their sides like piglets suckling a sow.

My uncle dropped anchor in the place that had been
given him before. Then he summoned me and Ve-Lo, his
commander of seamen, to accompany him ashore.

"Do not think it strange," he said, "that these folk neither gaze across the water at our vessel nor come out to
greet us. By their mannerly ethic, such would be im-
proper, making us feel conspicuous and ill at ease. When
we come to the house of the Wise Ones who are to them
such as an Initiate is to us, they will greet us as old acquaintances, stopped in at the door upon a daily stroll.
There will be no clamor and no hustle. Do you conduct
yourselves in like manner."

So it was that we slipped quietly into the gemlike town
that curved about the bay, tethering our cutter at the
longest jetty, which was placed before the door of a low
house built of polished stone that glittered in the sun of
the forenoon. My uncle walked easily to the round-
topped doorway and touched a little frame from which
translucent shells were suspended. They tinkled together,
making a fairy music, and a voice from within said,
"Enter, friends, and welcome."

Ro-Van stooped to clear the low doorframe, though Ve-

Lo and I could walk upright beneath it. A light curtain of veiling covered the inner door, for keeping out insects, I supposed, and we held it aside and went into the room, which seemed lined with mother-of-pearl, so light and gleaming were its walls. Upon a cool blue mat beside a window sat a man and a woman with scrolls in their hands and ink and pens upon low tables at their sides.

They set aside their work and rose to greet us, motioning us to sit with them upon the mats that they produced from a chest beneath the window. Their manner was unhurried and their bearing gentle as they settled again like two gray-clad butterflies upon their mat and touched a bell that swung beneath a table. At once a little serving maid entered, bearing a tray with steaming two-handled cups and little cakes and a covered pot upon it.

"It is a pleasure to find you well, Lo-Nee, Tu-Vrah," said my uncle. "Upon a fair morning it is well to sit and talk with friends."

"Indeed," said the woman, Lo-Nee, trilling our tongue strangely. "We look with particular joy upon your face today. We have found much use for the artifacts that you were so kind as to give us, in return for our unworthy handicrafts. And our merchants, though unused to trading afar, have used your golden coins to much advantage in trading with vessels that visit us from the southern seas. It is well that you ventured the dreadful passage to the west, though it grieves us that you must face such danger."

Then I knew that these people, courteous as they were, were also sensible and straightforward in trading. I slipped my little pouch of gold into my uncle's pocket, and he whispered to me that I might go and amuse myself in the town while the tedious process of trading was underway. So I went, Mip upon my shoulder, out into the mosaic pathways that served as roads for the island people.

Much was there to see and to hear. The houses were all of polished stone, but of different shapes and hues, set about the curving paths as jewels in a bracelet. Many people were about, now that we were safely ashore, and their musical voices greeted me, though I could not easily understand their words. Yet they smiled more often than they frowned, and I was well content.

At the farthest point of the curve that was the bay a stream came down from tree-greened heights to pass through the town on its way to reach the sea. Across this was spun a delicate bridge, all arching grace, webbed beneath with a filigree of bracing. It was so very beautiful that I did not, for a moment, see that another stood upon it as I climbed to the top.

The stream, touched with that strange blue which was the color of the waters of the ocean, frothed beneath the bridge, and in the quiet eddy protected by the buttress of the bridge swam two swans, gazing at their rippled reflections with royal disdain. I watched them in delight, leaning on the railing.

A quiet voice at my elbow said, "Do not lean too far, my friend. The waters of En-La are cold and deep, for all their innocent behavior. And those kingly birds are not above tweaking your hair or battering you under with their wings, given the opportunity."

Then I turned and saw her for the first time. Her eyes were bright with amusement, and her face was still and round as a pond into which no rain has ever fallen. My young heart, which had never done more than circulate my blood, gave a mad thump. Almost I thought that she might have heard, but she said nothing, only smiled and took my hand, leading me to the other side of the bridge to look into the mossy pool trapped upstream by the embankment.

"I love the golden minnows—see how they flicker in the light. My name is Su-La, and I come here each morning on my way to the meadows and drop crumbs of my breakfast bread to them. But never do I feed those arrogant swans! They are cold and heartless creatures."

Then I laughed aloud, and Mip, on my shoulder, gave an annoyed squeak. Su-La looked up, then stood on tiptoe and danced with excitement. "What lovely creature is this? Will he let me hold him?"

So I took Mip's clinging hands from my collar and soothed him, letting her tickle his chin and scratch his back. At last his suspicion was allayed, and he sat upon her shoulder with his long tail curled under her chin like a plume from some strange headdress. She was like a child in her delight, though she must have been very nearly my own age.

That was such a morning as comes but once, in the clear-souled flood of youth. My uncle readily gave me permission to go with Su-La into the meadows, where she tended her family's cattle as they grazed, seeing that none strayed into the dangerous heights where loose stones and clinging creepers would mean broken legs and lost meat and milk for her folk. There being no great hazard there for two-legged folk, we climbed, we two, to a moss-laden rock that thrust itself out from the cliffside, overlooking the little valley that was the grazing ground.

There we sat watching the kine and the town and the blue waters beyond, talking, talking with zest and laughter. Great amusement we knew in finding common terms for the things we saw, piecing our meanings from our dissimilar pronunciations, finding a language we could both

understand. You may smile, but long it was before we
discovered the most delightful language of all, which we
learned together, without words, with the most innocent
joy.

Then, lying in the westering sun, we smiled together
and knew that nothing must ever part us two. Su-La sat
up at last and reached for the little basket that she had
brought. Therefrom she took a parcel of little cakes and
spread them upon her kerchief.

"In our place," she said shyly, "when two find love,
they make a pledge. If we prick our fingers with my hair-
pin and let the blood drop onto a cake, thus"—and she
stabbed her fingertip with the shining point and let the
bright blood fall—"and then eat, each of us, a cake
enriched with the heart blood of the other, never will we
give our hearts to any other lover, however long we live."

I took the pin and, in turn, pricked my thumb and saw
the red drip onto a cake. Then each of us took up the
other's cake and ate, looking deep, deep, my gray eyes
into her green, and a part of our souls mingled for all of
time.

Too soon, the sun reached the edge of the sea, and we
must scramble down from our corner of the Land Beyond
the Sky and belabor the reluctant cattle until they moved
slowly toward home. We followed them out of the valley,
over the wooded ridge, down to their byre, which was
tucked snugly into a thicket of trees. Then we went, hand
in hand, down the gemmed path to the bridge where we
had met a thousand years before, that morning.

I found my uncle quietly pleased with the course of his
tradings, and determined that I should ask him that
night, as soon as his supper was completed, the proper
course to take concerning my newfound love.

Gravely he heard me, without a frown or a smile. Nodding sagely, he said, "You are of an age to give your heart, and you are one who loves with the mind as well. Yet all is not smooth in this. You are of the world of the Purple Waters, she of the Blue. Your father and mother wait in loneliness for your return. Would you remain here, however fair the land and perfect the love, and leave them childless and hopeless in their latter years? Think on this.

"Too, I was entrusted with your well-being and promised your safe return. Consider, for you are just, how it must be for me if I return to Shar-Nuhn alone and must find words to soften for your parents the fact that you chose to abandon them."

We sat in silence for a time, and I thought upon his words. They were fair, and he was in the right. Yet how could I leave Su-La when we had but begun to know the flower of joy?

"Let us go now to meet the people of your love. She, too, has a hard decision to make and loving parents to consider," my uncle said presently. This seemed wise, and we went ashore and sought out the house of Leh-To, the father of Su-La.

Theirs was a modest house, set well away from the bay. A light shone above the door, as if to welcome us, and I touched the door chimes only an instant before the door opened and Su-La stood there. She gazed into the eyes of my uncle, and he returned her regard. Then both smiled, as if they found much to respect and to like. My heart grew warm with love for both, but I struggled to preserve a sober face.

Her people were pleasant folk, sobered by the present problem yet with faces tracked with the lines of kindliness and thought. No other child had they, only Su-La, and their hearts were wrapped about her. Yet no word did they speak to sway her mind. Her joy gave them joy, and the disturbance of her tranquillity pained them.

"Greatly do I wish that I might linger here, giving these young folk time to examine their hearts," said my uncle, when we were seated and had exchanged pleasantries. "This voyage, by necessity, must be accomplished within a limited span of time, for we must return through the strait ere the ice comes, making the passage impossible for many months. Therefore their decisions must be made tomorrow, for upon the morning after, we must set sail once more. My nephew, as you have found for yourselves, is no light and reckless youngling, to be ordered by those older than he. The decision must be his. For all our sakes, I pray that both these children think long and well."

Leh-To nodded, taking the hand of his wife. "Thus it is with our child, also. What her inner self determines to be, that will we accept. Let your nephew go again tomorrow to the meadows, that they may have one day of happiness. Together they may find more easily the answers that will do justice to both." Then my eyes stung, though I fiercely refused to blink. I thanked them, and we took our leave.

The next day was all beauty—with a difference. The gray thread of loss lay underneath the love and the laughter, for both of us, without asking, knew the only answer. We savored each sunny minute, dreading its loss. We absorbed the sun, the breezes, the cries of birds, and the lowing of the kine with desperate attention, seeking to make them part of our very flesh. And at the end of day we said good-bye, without tears or lamentations.

The next morning we sailed upon the early tide, leaving Mip to comfort her heart. And nevermore have I given my heart to any, save in friendship.

* * *

Si-Lun said nothing, but looked far into the horizon.

Kla-Noh sat upon his coil of rope and leaned against the mast, and his old eyes never sought the eastern sky.

IX

A Quaking of Merchants

The night wind moved softly in the skies above Shar-Nuhn, and the city slept as peacefully as any seaport ever may. On the quay beside the black bulks of warehouses some few sailors staggered or slept, and the night watch prowled alertly in the ways of the city.

In the house of Kla-Noh there was deep silence and rest, and only the lipping of waves below his terrace broke the peace of the night. The little moon, Ralias, was rising, and the great moon, To-Sen, was at zenith, silvering the tops of the Purple Waters and turning the foam to pearl.

But there came, gradually as if from a distance, a dim growling from the heart of the earth below the city. It grew in strength, and the waters of the bay began to quiver as though little ripples were running crisscross the waves. The house of Kla-Noh groaned softly among its stones, and the old Seeker opened his eyes and listened to the night.

As he lay quietly, he heard a tap at the door of his chamber.

"Come in, Si-Lun," he whispered, and the door opened upon the shape of his foster son and companion. "Have you felt the motion of the lands?" the old man asked, sitting up and reaching for his robe.

"Aye," answered the younger. "The land seems, however gently, troubled to its foundations. And that reminds me—and you—of a certain inscription that we have seen upon a door in the Tower of Truth."

"My thought, O son-in-heart. Some Adept is troubling Shar-Nuhn, and you may be sure it is none of the Shar-Neen who speaks the spell upon the ground of home. Let us go out upon the terrace, that we may feel the night." Kla-Noh tied the girdle of his robe and took the arm of the young man.

The moons rode in serenity above the strangely wrinkled waters. Shar-Nuhn seemed undisturbed, and no motion could be seen upon the land, but the faint growling persisted as a throb in the bones of the two Seekers. Long they stood, but the unrest grew faint and fainter yet and was, at length, altogether gone. Then they turned and went back to their rest, knowing that the morning would bring change.

Some there were within the city who knew no rest that night. The drunken men noticed no tremor more than their own. The sleeping never woke, so gentle was the motion. But the guilty started upright at the first movement and lay in agony of spirit until the first light liberated them from their couches. Then they gathered at the Inn of Crimson Fishes to decide upon their course.

So it was that Kla-Noh and Si-Lun, busy about their midmorning tasks, heard a tapping at the door that drew the padding feet of Nu-Veh in answer. The Seekers looked at each other and smiled. The door opened and Nu-Veh peered into the chamber. "Many merchants of the city have come to your door, O wise Kla-Noh. They

wish to take council with you. O-Lat, the chief of merchants, begs that you speak with them."

The old Seeker's eyes narrowed. "So the merchants of
Shar-Nuhn bestir themselves in the forenoon and hurry to
my house," he murmured. "A strange twist of circum-
stance. Tell them that I will attend them in the chamber
of study, Nu-Veh. Show them there and say that I will attend them soon."

He turned to Si-Lun. "They will speak more frankly
with me alone, for they know me of old. Do you sit in the
antechamber and open your spirit to the emanations of
theirs. I will hear their words, you their hearts' sensa-
tions. Between us, we may arrive at more than truth."

It was a strangely subdued huddle of men who greeted
the old man in his study. None is more pitiable than one
suddenly shorn of the arrogance of power, and there sat
seven in that state. Their eyes avoided his, their hands
were extended toward his grasp in the most hesitating
manner. They exuded guilt as though they were a pack of
mischievous children and not the wielders of wealth and
influence who had made Shar-Nuhn great among nations.

Kla-Noh motioned for them to sit, then sat himself.
"How come the great of Shar-Nuhn to my door so early
and in such humbled condition?" he asked mildly. "Can it
be that the . . . unrest . . . of the night has disturbed
you?"

O-Lat rose suddenly, his gray eyes sparking with
anger, but he recollected himself and sat again before answering, "We are concerned, truly, Seeker. We are . . .
undecided as to what course we should follow in this
matter." Then, as though unwilling to continue in such
placating vein, he closed his lips and shook his head.

His fellows leaned toward him, and a mutter of talk

rose from the group, but O-Lat continued to shake his head, and at last Re-Nil, second-wealthiest merchant of Shar-Nuhn, spoke.

"We are come, Kla-Noh, to lay before you our fear and our guilt. Yea, guilt," he said sternly, as those about him murmured in protest. He drew his deep-green robe about his thin shoulders and stood. "We have followed our bent, which has made ours the richest city upon our planet. We have traded with those near and those afar, sending our fleets to all parts of the world that they may reach. We have garnered rich stuffs in the Far Islands and sold them to the folk of Lirith in Kyrannon. Our vessels have even followed in the track of your uncle and dared the terrible Strait of the Far Continent, going into the Blue Waters upon its other side. We have been diligent in the enrichment of our city—and ourselves.

"Yet one city there has been that would have none of our goods, would sell us none of theirs. It sits, not far distant, upon the rough coasts to the south, and all the gemwork that is the glory of the city of Shan-Lith goes to merchants of the Far Continent. From the bowels of their mountains the Shan-Leeth dig jewels of strangest fire. They polish and cut them into unutterably brilliant forms. They set them in precious metals as delicate as lace. But they sell none to us.

"Many delegations have we sent to them, seeking to make an agreement for trade, but none would they honor with their attention. Then, months ago, we received word from the Anun of Shan-Lith, for so their ruler is called, as they have no Initiates and no Towers of Truth. He offered a trade, if we were willing once again to send spokesmen to attend him. This we did speedily, you may be sure, though I was not chosen to go with those sent.

"Our folk returned in distress of mind. One thing, and

that alone, would induce the Anun to allow his people to
trade with us. He sought the Second Secret of Shar-Nuhn
as the price. It seemed a strange thing to wish for, to us.
Any of us may go at will to the Tower and obtain the two
lesser secrets of Shar-Nuhn. True, the Second Secret is
hedged about with safeguards and instructions that the
Initiates make clear to us, for the power to trouble the
lands to their foundations is a dread one. Yet none has
ever been denied it, at need.

"So we sought out one of our fellows, who is a scholar,
to ask of him the secret, which he had learned as a matter
of curiosity in his youth. He was in doubt that our purpose was worthy, but we showed him the possibilities for
profit to all of the city, and he agreed that harm should
not come of so good a project.

"Oh, that he had been right, or that we had been
wiser!

"We have been safe in the keeping of the Initiates for
many ages of men, and we have forgotten that there are
those who live by other standards than ours." The old
man held his sleeve before his face, and Kla-Noh leaned
forward and touched his shoulder.

"So you gave the Anun the Second Secret, hiding from
your own eyes the baseness of your cause. And the Anun
has tested his new power . . . upon Shar-Nuhn herself.
And that, my unwise friends, has showed to you the purpose that he held in his heart," the old Seeker said meditatively.

"True, woefully true," sighed Re-Nil. "By our own act
we have delivered our city over to its enemy. We should
go at once to the Initiates . . . but you see with what
trembling and quaking we come before you, who are the
most unassuming of men. How can we, then, stand before
the Initiates, who taught us the ways of virtue, and tell

them that wc have sold our city for the right to barter
gauds in the marketplaces of the world?"

The Seeker smiled. "Do you think that they, who hold
the key to wisdom, never walked in the world and lived
as do others of our kind? No man or woman of their number has not erred, even as have you and I, from greed or
lust or lack of judgment. They do not judge, and they do
not lay blame upon those who seek them out for aid.
They leave such things in the laps of the gods and turn
their own hands to helping those who have need. But I
will go to them in your stead, for such is your desire. Return to your warehouses and wait. But do not count your
wealth on this day. Count those things which have been
imperiled by your act, and pray to the gods that they are
not lost to us all."

Hardly had the merchants gone from sight when Kla-
Noh called to Si-Lun to prepare their vessel for a swift
tack across the Bay of Shar-Nuhn to the Tower of Truth.
And before those merchants were again seated at their
places in the countinghouses the two Seekers were upon
the Purple Waters in the perilous pitching of waves that
set in dire currents about the foot of the Tower.

At their hail, the little door at the base of the great
steps was opened, and they anchored their vessel and
trusted themselves to their small boat to reach the entry-
way, for much danger attended upon the approach to the
steps that led up into the upper Tower. To their surprise,
Ru-Anh, the Father of Initiatcs, met them as they hurried
in, damp and gasping from the spray of their passage.

"We have awaited a coming," he said, taking their wet
cloaks and hanging them upon pegs. "But little did we
think to see Kla-Noh and Si-Lun. Your errand must be urgent, for never have you sought us upon matters of little
weight. Yet our questions seek answers, also—"

"Our needs are the same," interrupted Kla-Noh, shaking the damp from his beard. "We are come in the stead of the mischief-makers who caused the tremor felt in the night. And sore is their misdeed, make no mistake. They quake in their places of business, counting their sins and full of shame at their lack of courage. Me they could face, for they know me to be a sinner of long standing, like themselves. They could not bring themselves to stand before you to confess their unwisdom, so I am come, with Si-Lun."

They were entering the great chamber of consultation as he spoke, and he paused to make a bow to the group of Initiates assembled there, their blue robes making a celestial glimmer move upon the polished stone of the walls. But motion ceased when Kla-Noh stood forth and told his story. The silence of attention gave way to the silence of thought when his words came to an end.

Among the Initiates there was little need for speech, so keenly honed were the edges of their spirits. What one thought and held forth in the front of his mind the others knew. The Seekers, with their questing spirits sharpened by study and effort, felt whispers of thought flit by like bat wings in a cave, and they could follow a little of the suggestion and countersuggestion that flowed between their companions.

At length the rustle of unvoiced thought subsided, and Ru-Anh rose and raised his hand. "Again, it seems, we must call upon our friends to do what we may not. For"— and he turned to the Seekers in explanation—"we, as the sole governing body of Shar-Nuhn, cannot send any of our number into the realm of the Anun of Shan-Lith without specific invitation. This he is unlikely to extend to us, in the light of his intent toward us.

"But someone—or two—must go into the southern lands

to wrest the Second Secret back from those who would, and will, misuse it against us and against others. And we must ask you again, Kla-Noh and Si-Lun, to be our help in time of need."

The Seekers knew that they need not speak, but they bowed their heads in assent. Then Ru-Anh took their hands in his and raised them to their feet.

"Let us go into my chambers, where we may sit and talk at ease," he said. "Much there is to tell you; there are many instructions that you will need, many secrets."

For all their long experience gleaned in their active lives, never had Kla-Noh and Si-Lun dreamed of the existence of the skills and instruments that were revealed to them in the next hours. They were taught, as well as might be done in so short a span of time, to function as Initiates, with the store of wisdom of the entire order at their command. Their delight as scholars was hardly outweighed by their concern for the city, and many a wistful glance they cast at volumes and instruments that were not needful for their present purpose. Yet they mastered their curiosity and set themselves to learn all that was needed in the recovery of the Second Secret.

So it was that, when dawn touched the Purple Waters on the third day of their stay in the Tower, they were declared to be ready, and Ru-Anh laid his hands upon their heads and looked into their eyes.

"It is a difficult task that we have set for you, Seekers, and one that is no duty of yours. Only the goodwill of your hearts takes you upon this journey," he said. "Your vessel has been readied with all that you may have use for, and we have set your Shamal, Kla-Noh, in all our hands and looked into it with the force of our spirits, that its fires may be at their fullest strength, should you need to speak with us from afar.

"All that we may do with our hands has been done. But the might of our hearts will be with you as you go."

The two wrung his hands and raised their arms to salute others of the Initiates who had delayed their duties to bid them farewell. Then they went through the little portal into the skiff and made their way to the vessel, which swung at anchor as though anxious to be away. And when the anchor was aboard and the sails set, the craft danced away, out of the bay, and off across the Purple Waters toward the lands of the south.

The prayers of the Initiates held weight with the gods, the Seekers decided, for the winds held firmly from the north to speed their passage. Racks of cloud promised storm, but they knew that the power of the First Secret of Shar-Nuhn, which held the waters in calm, would smooth their way, that no time be lost in their journey. And truly, in six days they sighted the cleft peak that brooded above the city of Shan-Lith, and knew that they neared their goal.

Now Shan-Lith, unlike Shar-Nuhn, was set in no tranquil bay with ready access to the sea. The steep southern mountains tumbled headlong into the waves upon these coasts, and the miners who had founded the city in ages long forgotten had found a broad river that cut through the crags. A league or so upstream, a wide meadow set into the side of a slope gave them foothold, and there Shan-Lith grew, over the long years, into a great city, rich with the gleanings of the mountains and the crafts of its people.

Even more unlike Shar-Nuhn, whose bay was guarded by none save the gods and the Tower of Truth, the river mouth that approached Shan-Lith was fortified, and officials of the port must pass upon any vessel entering the river to seek the city. So it was that Kla-Noh and Si-

Lun, knowing the ways of the place from older times, made no appearance before the river but anchored their craft secretly in the lee of an islet, covering their masts with branches that no patrolling boat might discover her.

Their skiff bore them to shore in darkness, for clouds hid the moons. Skilled as they were, it took little time for them to hide their boat and take themselves up into the concealment of the heavy forests that marched down to the sea upon the shoulders of the mountains. Before dawn touched the edge of the sky, they were burrowed into a thicket where even the wild beasts could hardly know their presence.

They passed the day in sleep, for they knew that they must move after sunset if they were to reach their goal. But before they slept they lay silent for a time, hands gripped together, eyes tightly closed, feeling outward with a new skill, searching for the self of the Anun, that they might know in which direction to seek him. Many selves they found, some virtuous, more not, most simply the enduring animal, without complex thought. And at last they found the Anun, whose spirit cast a purple shadow and whose self-esteem was not dimmed, even in sleep.

Upon waking, Kla-Noh looked upon the charts that the Initiates had given them, marking upon one of them the direction in which they had found the Anun. The line he made bisected the city of Shan-Lith and lay across the center of the palace of the Anun.

"I had entertained hope," said Si-Lun, "that the Anun might have decided to ride abroad into the country for a time. Yet if the gods hold Shar-Nuhn in esteem, they will attend us. Ease has never seemed a part of the work of the gods, in truth."

His foster father chuckled. "Never have I found ease in

the tasks of gods or men," he said. "But this will be a labor to match any I have seen, for we must seek out the Anun in his house, amid his guards. And tyrants fear many things and employ men to protect them and men to watch the men who protect them and spies to oversee the lot. I think that we shall use the Shamal, very gently, just to inform our friends that we have arrived and are about to begin. Take my hand, O son-in-heart."

The two grasped hands and sat, backs to a tree, as Kla-Noh warmed the Shamal in his other palm and gazed into it deeply. Soon the topaz jewel began to burn with internal light, and from it came a whisper: ". . . we are here . . . we are here . . . we are here."

Then Kla-Noh spoke softly into the shimmer that was the heart of the Shamal. "The two who seek afar are arrived at their destination. We begin our work at sunset. Hold us in heart, brothers and sisters, for we go into peril."

The whispers paused for a heartbeat; then the tiny voice of Ru-Anh spoke from the jewel. "Our thought goes forth with you, Seekers. Go in trust, for the gods love no tyrant."

There was silence, and the gem dimmed to its native glimmer. The Seekers rose to their feet and stretched their stiff limbs before packing away their equipment. With long use, the waking of the Shamal was becoming less wearing upon them, so they felt none of the depletion that attended a long usage. Thus they were able to shoulder their packs and begin their scramble through the forest soon after eating their quick ration of food.

Often had Kla-Noh spoken of the weight of his years lying upon his bones, yet he went up through the forest as swiftly as did Si-Lun, sliding among the undergrowth, treading the thousand-year-deep forest mold under noiseless feet. The resinous scent of the trees filled them with joy as they moved in the shadow. The shadow became utter darkness all too soon, as the last light left the sky, and Si-Lun kindled a lightglass, that they might see their direction crystal and keep to their course.

They knew that they must climb the outer face of the seaward mountain, making certain that they descended its inner slope on the riverward side. Keeping to the ridge above the river, they would then be able to approach the city without going among the outlying houses and farms that lined the valley. The league that lay between the city and the sea would be doubled for them, but they hoped to reach their goal before dawn.

It was no simple thing to do in strange country, nightbound, in secrecy. And after crossing to the cityward side of the prominence, they could risk their lightglass in only the most necessary places, for they knew that watch was kept upon the heights by patrols that skirted the city by day and by night. Yet so secretly and cannily did they go that few were the birds that muttered a sleepy query, and only two prowling beasts had their hunting troubled by their passing.

Upon the inland way they found their steps guided by the leaden glimmer of the river far below them. Even beneath a clouded sky the wide waters caught the little light of the hidden moons, and they found the intermittent glimpses that they caught through the tree boles a help in finding their way. When they progressed farther still, they could see the lamps of the city and its outlying districts.

Even in the middle hours of the night, Shan-Lith seemed busy, its streets well lit by torches flaring over almost every doorpost, its wharves abustle with porteurs

loading and unloading vessels that hailed from strange
ports and flew unknown banners. The Seekers paused for
a time upon their high perch, considering the shape of
the city, comparing their map with its guiding lines
against the actuality below them.

Being built in the midst of mountains of stone, the city
itself seemed of a piece with its surrounding peaks, for
the same stone shaped its craggy buildings. No ease of
curve or grace of line was there, as in Shar-Nuhn. The
stern land and the strong wills of the builders were
reflected in the square and uncompromising bulks. In its
center, rising in the shape of a stepped pyramid, stood
the house of the Anun, its pale stone glimmering ruddy in
the light of the street torches. And even from the height
the Seekers could see the movement of antlike guards
about it.

Yet they set off down the steep forest without hesita-
tion, and when they emerged into the open they found
themselves in a quiet area of homes whose inhabitants
were soundly asleep, it seemed, as no chink of light
showed about door or window. Had the sleepers been sitting in their doorways, however, they might well have
missed the softly passing figures of the dark-clad Seekers,
who neither hastened nor paused but went through the
dim lanes as though they knew them of old.

But when they emerged into the more central part of
the city they began passing many folk who seemed to be
hurrying upon urgent affairs, though the hour was that
when Shar-Nuhn would have been most deeply asleep.
Brighter grew the streets, more numerous the people in
them, and now the Seekers began to feel the pressure of
eyes upon their backs, and they knew that something
about their dress or bearing was arousing curiosity.

Finding a colonnaded place centered by a fountain and filled with welcome shadow, the two disappeared into it gratefully and surveyed one another.

"Do my senses misguide me, or have all those we passed been short men and women with dark skin and darker hair?" asked Si-Lun, gazing down at his long legs with dismay.

"Such are the folk of Shan-Lith," answered Kla-Noh. "But so well frequented has its port ever been that all manner of folk could walk in the streets without remark. The new Anun may well have wrought more changes than that concerning Shar-Nuhn. And if we are the only outlanders abroad, we may find ourselves questioned or taken before we may complete our task. Yet I hesitate to use the secrets of the Initiates with less than great need as reason."

Si-Lun looked again down his own length of limb. "Our skins we might darken, and our hair could be hidden in headcloths, for some such I saw on those upon the street. But though you might stoop enough to pass, there is no hope for me. And should a torch show some passerby my green eyes or your gray ones, that would betray us, too. It seems that the time has come to use the dark jewel, that we may walk unseen."

Kla-Noh sighed, but he nodded and slipped his pack from his shoulders. From a leathern bag he drew forth a black crystal, cut square and faceted: the Shanoth. Drawing together, the Seekers held the glinting gem so that all their four hands touched some part of it. Their eyes they fixed upon one another, but their thoughts touched the jewel, even as did their fingers, caressing its image within their minds. They stood, frozen in concentration, for many heartbeats, straining to apply the things that the Initiates had taught them for use of the Shanoth.

"You are fading, my friend and father," Si-Lun remarked at last. "As a fog in the sunlight, you are quietly going away. I had not known that we would not be able to see each other."

"Only the mad may see us now," answered Kla-Noh. "No man in his wits may know us near, unless he touch us. And that is a peril which we must avoid. Farewell to my sight, O son-in-heart, until we again take the jewel into our hands."

Then the jewel floated magically, it seemed, into its bag and the bag into the pack and the pack was lifted . . . and disappeared. And then a hand touched Si-Lun's arm, and Kla-Noh said musingly, "It is as well we do not lose each other, as we cannot go calling invisibly through the streets."

So they went out again into the ways and felt no more glances. And now they had opportunity to notice the strangeness of the city. In Shar-Nuhn, at this hour, they would have encountered some few sailors, uplifted or downcast by drink, singing in doorways or weeping in gutters. No such could be seen here. The tavern entrances were dark and no song or laughter poured forth. The doors sagged on their hinges and long disuse had festooned them with cobwebs.

The Seekers began to study the faces of those they met on the way, peering into approaching countenances until those so spied upon began to shift their eyes uneasily, seeking the source of the gaze they felt. And the Seekers saw that the faces of the people were worn and unhappy, though they seemed well fed enough and warmly clothed. Not one quirk of smile could be seen, not one satisfied expression.

The pressure of Kla-Noh's hand on his arm drew Si-Lun into the doorway of one of the neglected taverns, where they stepped carefully over the fallen door leaf into the empty room beyond.

"No comely city is this," grunted Kla-Noh as he seated himself, raising a puff of dust that showed his companion where he had alighted.

Si-Lun drew a chair to the table and sat, his elbows making strange dimples in the accumulation of debris that had covered its top. "These folk have the look of those under a tyrant's rule," he assented. "Were you ever in this place before? Has it been in any way thus?"

"The old Anun was a stern man, quick to anger, harsh in his judgments, but no tyrant," answered the old man. "The laws of the city were his rule, and he would temper them for none, but he also lived by them and did not seek to seize what he had no authority to have. He had no son, when last I knew of him, and was of an age to make it unlikely that he ever might. This Anun may be a nephew or even one who reached out when no other hand was ready to seize power when the old man died. He died, I have heard, quickly, without illness to give warning, and seemingly in the fullness of health."

"So the city is beset by its ruler, and the folk in the streets walk with tears in their hearts and sorrow on their faces," mused Si-Lun. "It may be that the Initiates will be interested. So busy are they with those whose world moves between their hands, they seldom look abroad to see who may need aid and counsel."

"It may be that we may accomplish more than we were sent to do," agreed Kla-Noh. "But the night is going, and we must go also."

So they made their way back onto the street and, hastening now, moved toward the central way of the city where stood the house of the Anun. The torches grew more numerous along the edges of the walkway, and the

Seekers moved into the center of the street in order to diminish their betraying shadows. They were taking care to make no sound as they walked and they dared not even to whisper, for the ways were becoming thronged with laden laborers bearing bundles and bales from the dockside to the warehouses.

Suddenly Si-Lun felt eyes upon his back. He started with alarm and squeezed his arm to his side, pressing the hand of Kla-Noh, that he might take warning. Both stopped and looked back. Behind them stood a ragged child who gazed at them with great curiosity. Her face was grimed and bruised, as though with harsh treatment, and her thin arms were bare to the night's chill. But her eyes told the tale, for they were set in that faraway gaze that denotes a troubled mind.

As they stood in the street, wondering what was best to do, a burdened man passed them and stopped to look at the child.

"What do you here, mindless one? Take yourself out of the way of honest folk. If your people do not keep you closely, we shall send for the Protectors, and they'll deal with you," he said harshly, elbowing her aside.

"But I am looking at the strange men!" she cried. "See them—they are tall and fair."

With an ugly laugh, the man moved away. "You have seen no tall fair men since you lay in your mother's arms, for no such are allowed now in the city. But you have also seen, you say, the Dark Folk of the Mountains. Go away, madling, to your place," he called back to her.

But the child still stood staring until the Seekers went on their way, and she followed them at a distance, peering with her dim-lit eyes as though even she saw them only by flickers.

This by no means made for ease of spirit. Though none

whom they passed even paused to look at their follower, still her presence weighed upon them and her glance seemed to point them out as though it were a beam of light cast upon them. But still they moved, cautiously and with speed, through the streets until they arrived at the house of the Anun.

There they met with a check, even in their invisible state. About the wide terraces that fell in stepped layers to the level of the way moved lines of guards in dark cloaks, and their swords bore the sheen of much use. Across the width of the great doorway at the top of broad steps there stood a solid line of men with pikes held upright before them. There seemed little space to move between them, even for one who was both invisible and intangible.

Standing close beside a wall, uncomfortably aware of the stare of the child focused upon them, pondering, the Seekers paused. Then Si-Lun felt warm breath at his ear, and the voice of Kla-Noh breathed, "We must use the second of the jewels. I cannot make it visible to you, but you must direct your thought toward it. Here is my hand —hold yours upon it and feel the gem between, keeping in your memory its green glow as we saw it in the Tower. Will the men before us into standing, wide-eyed sleep. Come. . . ."

And they froze into concentration, seeing nothing save the green blaze of the Shalith, thrusting with all their wills through its strange facets at the senses of the men upon the door slab.

Time froze about them, they felt, as they sent the flame of their spirits into the heart of the jewel. And, unseen, the power they fed into it rayed outward. They could feel the resistance of the air and the flesh and wills of men, but still they strained at their task. Inch by foot by yard, the influence of the Shalith moved until it reached the men arrayed across the doorway at the terrace top. And when their senses congealed into sleep, the Seekers knew.

With deep sighs and aching heads they relaxed their impulse. The image of the gem faded from their minds, and they moved toward the Anun's house. They were not followed, for the child had been within the radius of the Shalith and stood sleeping with the rest of those upon the way.

With speed the Seekers fled up the steps and into the unguarded portal. They knew that behind them those who had slept for those precious seconds would be waking again to their work, never knowing that some heartbeats of their lives had been pilfered from them.

The halls of the great house lay in shadow, for only a dim lamp or lightglass burned at intervals down their lengths. Few servants moved, and those seemed half asleep, so the two made good speed through the lower parts of the house. The wide stair curved upward at the end of a lateral passage. Its dark height stretched away into the upper reaches of the building, and they could see that the candles which had provided light had guttered in their sconces and died away until the whole stairwell was a gulf of shadow.

Kla-Noh reached beside him, feeling for Si-Lun. When his fingers touched the young man's arm, he said softly, "Let us go up, and then we may return ourselves to the sight of men. For our work now will be such that we will need to look eye into eye and to place palm unerringly into palm."

They stole up the stair swiftly, meeting no one, hearing nothing save a deep thud from somewhere below, as though an unwary guard had drifted into sleep and dropped his lance. Quietly they went, and when they

reached the top of the stair they found themselves in a
long and dim-lit hall lined with closed and silent doors.

Kla-Noh dared a whisper. "The first door to the right.
It is a chance, truly, but something tells me that the room
behind that one door is vacant this night. Come, son-in-
daring, let us resume our shapes."

The door opened to pressure on the latch peg, and the
two Seekers found themselves in a chamber so dark that
invisibility was unimportant. There was a scritching
sound, and Si-Lun found himself staring into the globe of
a lightglass that hung in the midst of the air, until it was
set gently upon a small chest.

"Now," said the voice of Kla-Noh, "I shall take the
Shanoth again in my hand. Think upon it, Si-Lun, as will
I. Place your hands here upon mine, which are beside the
lightglass. Now . . . think. . . ."

Once again they visualized the dark gem, the refracted
flickers of its facets, the mystery that was its heart. Then
they were beginning to see that which they had only
remembered, as the gem began to shimmer into that
order of existence which was discernible to the eyes of
men. The hands of the two now curdled palely into view,
and soon they stood in their own shapes, gladdening each
the eyes of the other.

A step in the hall without brought them to instant attention. The lightglass was quenched as though it had
never shone, and the Seekers found the wall behind the
now-opening door.

A shout interrupted the door's swing. "What do you
here, child? The house of the Anun is no place of yours!
Get you gone into the streets, where your proper place is,
or I'll give you over to the Protectors."

The hidden two could hear the voice of the mad child
of the streets as she answered, "I follow the strange men.

I slept for a little, and they were gone, but I know they came here, for I feel it. Let me go with them!"

"There is a fate in this," said Kla-Noh clearly. "The gods are working, and we must aid their task."

He pulled the door wide and stood looking into the hall. The child gaped at him, then smiled and said, "Now I can see you well. Before, you came and went like shadows in firelight."

"Aye," said Kla-Noh. Then he stepped into the hall and confronted the servant who stood there with terror upon her face. From his pouch he took the Shalith and held it to his forehead.

Still as a man of stone he stood, holding the greenly pulsing jewel to his head, his gaze skewering the petrified servant as would a beam of light. Her face went slack, her eyes dulled, and she sank into a heap by the wall.

"She will not wake for hours," said the old Seeker. "We must put her safely by, and this chamber seems well enough for our purpose. Take her by the heels, Si-Lun, and we will bear her to the couch."

It was quickly done. Then Si-Lun knelt beside the child and said, "Little one, we go upon a task of much gravity, much danger, but one that is the work of the gods. Come with us if you must, but keep silent and hide yourself when we bid you to. Even you may have some labor to accomplish, before we are done."

Then he took her hand and followed his foster father down the hall to a great door, studded with iron bands and decorated with golden scrolls. Before it stood two guards, dozing inside their helms. They woke instantly at the sound of heels upon the flooring, but Kla-Noh again beamed the strength of the Shalith upon each in turn, and they sank into deeper sleep, leaning against the wall, propped upright by their lances.

The leaves of the door opened with a gusty sigh, and the three filed in, closing and barring the entrance behind them. They found themselves in an antechamber where slept four men upon four fur-clothed couches. But not one wakened as they tiptoed past, holding their breaths and watching closely that they trod upon no dropped helm or sword and kicked against no low table.

At the end of the chamber was a door swathed in crimson draperies worked in golden and silver threads with the emblem of the Anun. But that ancient emblem, Kla-Noh found upon looking closely, had been altered. The peak was there, for the mountain above the city, with the circle touching its foot to show the existence of the city. The silver line that stood for the river was there also. But a new device had been added: a black sword lay diagonally across the entire design.

"A sinister device," whispered the old man to himself. "A sinister Anun has made it. We are not a heartbeat too early in beginning our work."

The door was locked. Only a most untrusting man indeed must lie beyond it, Si-Lun thought, as he knelt to examine the catch. With his dagger blade he managed to slip the metal tongue of the catch from its groove. Then he jabbed the sharp point into the wooden bar within the chamber and levered it a tiny bit backward. Again and again he gained that little span. At last the bar was free, and the door sighed softly open.

Only when it was closed and barred behind them did the three remember again to breathe. But their breaths caught in their throats as they gazed at the great couch before them. It also was swathed in crimson, but this was worked in a pattern of swords, black and gold and silver and green, crossed and parallel, single and in pairs, a mad array of patterns without logic or overall design.

Upon the couch lay a thin figure wrapped in fur. As
they stood gazing at him, he woke and turned in a single
motion. The sight of three strangers within his most
highly guarded place seemed to stupefy the Anun for a
long moment. Then he spoke in a strangled voice.

"Who comes in the deep of night to my bedside? Are
you humankind or specters? Speak to me. . . . Do I
dream?"

"No bodiless stalkers of the night are we," answered
Kla-Noh. "Nor are we enemies to any save those who are
the enemies of the gods.

"We are come from Shar-Nuhn."

Hearing those words, the Anun cowered down among
his furs, and by their quivering they knew that he quaked
for his life. "No enemy am I of Shar-Nuhn," his muffled
voice declared. "Your merchants bartered with me, and I
but tested to find if their spell was worthy. No ill do I in-
tend your city, nor any else upon this world. Go you to
your own place and leave me to my sleep."

The child had watched with her strange and flickering
gaze as the conversation progressed. Now she spoke. "He
will spring up and seize a sword that is beneath his
bolster," she said. "He has a dagger, but he thinks it isn't
long enough."

Then Si-Lun made a great leap and flung himself
across the muffled figure of the Anun, holding him
trapped among his coverings while Kla-Noh tore down a
golden rope from the hangings and sought his feet and
arms to bind them fast.

When they had fettered him and set him upright, they
sat and rested for a space, while their captive sought des-
perately to shout past the cloth that they had tied round
his mouth.

"Believe that we mean you no harm, to body or spirit.

Only good do we bring to you," said Si-Lun, passing his hand wearily over his face. "The Initiates are no dealers in assassination and destruction, and from them we come, though we are only Seekers After Secrets who serve them and the gods."

But the man's eyes glared wildly as though he had understood no word that was said. They roved about the room until they settled upon the child. Then the Anun jerked as though a blow had been dealt him, and he sagged against the end of the couch.

Kla-Noh rose and leaned above him, unfastening the gag. The Anun looked up at him, and there was no hope in his gaze or his voice when he spoke.

"How came you to know of her? None save the old Anun's most trusted servants knew, and them I slew when I took the power into my hands. How could I leave the city to such as she? Her lineage alone could not make her sane. And I was his adviser for many years, though little did he need one. Still, sometimes he listened to me, and much I learned from him—what to do and what not, as I saw him fumble among the powers in his hands, wasting opportunities that I could have seized.

"You can see that she was no fit ruler of Shan-Lith. Who else had more right than I to take what she could not use?"

He fell silent, and Kla-Noh bent low and looked into his face. "And did you send her into the streets to starve, knowing that she was mad? Little do you deserve the emblem of rulership. But you are here, and we must make what use of you we can. Still, you must know that we have powers you cannot understand, and it will serve you not at all to make outcry."

Then the old man unbound the man, and Si-Lun placed a chair before a low round table which he drew to the center of the room. There they placed the Anun. Then Kla-Noh reached once again into his pouch and drew forth a bag from which he took the principal jewel of all, the Shamal. He warmed its topaz glow between his palms, then laid it upon the table before the Anun.

"Look into the jewel," he told him. "Gaze deeply into its fires . . . see how they wax more golden every moment. Look into the gem!"

Si-Lun leaned forward, as did Kla-Noh, and all three stared into the stone, deeper and deeper, as though it were drawing them into itself. Then from the space about the Shamal came a whisper: "We are here. We are here. We are here. . . ."

"Here is he who needs the healing of your arts," said Kla-Noh. "And in healing him you will work great good for the city he rules. But there is another, child of the old Anun, who is deemed mad, yet she sees the truth that is before her, in flesh or in heart. Her also you must examine, for she is the Anunin of Shan-Lith. Yet I feel in my heart that she needs no cure, but only training."

"We hear," said the voice of Ru-Anh.

Then the Anun bent low over the Shamal, as though he sought to enter its amber-golden heart, and whispers rose about him. A beam of light shot from it and centered between his eyes. The tautness of his back began to ease, and his head rested between his hands as he absorbed the messages that flowed through the gem. At last he sank forward in sleep, and the whispers increased in volume.

"Bring the child," they said, and Si-Lun bore away the sleeping Anun to his couch while Kla-Noh put the child in the chair and showed her the jewel.

"Ohhh!" she cried, and she cupped her hands about the Shamal and gazed into it with delight. Then she listened with concentration to the whispers and, when they died

away, raised the jewel to her forehead and closed her
eyes. After a long moment she placed it again on the
table and turned to Kla-Noh.

"They wish for you now," she said, and her gaze was
filled with wonder.

"Bring the child to us," Ru-Anh said to the Seeker.
"She is no madling but one gifted with the true sight,
which seems a madness to ordinary men. She has had no
teaching, no affection, but this we can supply. With us
she will receive training and love, that she may return
one day to her country as, perhaps, its greatest ruler."

"And what of the present Anun?" asked the Seeker.
"Will he now turn to the ways of the gods?"

"Perhaps not wholly, but he will be better than he was.
We have set within his heart a barrier against cruelty and
callousness, and we have also showed to him a little of
the power that the gods have put into our hands. What
virtue will not do, fear will, for his is not a strong spirit."

With this, the whisper died away, and the Shamal
dimmed to its normal hue. Kla-Noh wrapped it again and
placed it in his pouch, then turned to Si-Lun.

"Rouse yonder man," he said. "We must have a writ of
passage in his hand and with his seal."

It was no easy task to awaken the Anun, and when
roused he seemed dazed. But another man looked from
his eyes when he was at last brought firmly to his senses.
A man less warped by ambition, less stunted by greed
seemed to be before them, and they were comforted to
think that this man would bring, perhaps, smiles again to
the faces of the folk of Shan-Lith.

The writ was easily asked and given, and, as they lifted
the bar of the door, he said, "It seems . . . perhaps I am
wrong, for I have been dreaming . . . but it seems that I
may owe you thanks. I believe that you have served me

well, though I cannot remember how. Fare you well and in safety, and come again to Shan-Lith."

"We will come again, perhaps, O Anun," said Kla-Noh. "Rule well and in happiness until we do."

Then the Seekers, leading the child by the hand, went out quietly through the sleeping house, past the astonished guards who could hardly credit the evidence of their eyes when they were shown the writ of passage, and out of the city, where many puzzled glances followed their progress.

Dawn found them upon the mountain, where they paused to rest, and midday saw them upon their vessel, anchors lifted, sails hoisted, ready to sail for Shar-Nuhn.

The child, through all, had followed without protest. Now she seemed all joy as she sat in the bow gazing ahead into the deeps of sky and sea, as though she knew what the end of the voyage would bring to her.

And the Seekers, weary to the bone, smiled upon one another as they worked the craft, and upon the child, and wondered within their spirits at the marvelous working-out of fate that they had seen.

X

The Door to Otherwhere

Kla-Noh lay upon his couch, gasping for breath. The hot wind from the west moved across his face, drying the perspiration clinging there, but it did little to cool him.

Si-Lun sat nearby, seeking to comfort his foster father by his presence and an occasional quiet word. Now he moved to lay a dampened cloth upon the old man's forehead, searching his countenance worriedly as he leaned above him.

"My friend and father," he said, as he returned to his chair, "for too long have you lain in illness. I beg you, let me summon an Initiate from the Tower of Truth. A healer you need, though you will not seek. In two short hours I could sail to the Tower and return with your old friend Ru-Anh, who would hasten to comfort you and to cool your fevers."

But Kla-Noh shook his head. Turning his eyes toward the window that opened upon the bay of Shar-Nuhn, he sighed. "No," he breathed, "I will not call. Great must be the anguish ere I trouble the Initiates in my own behalf. If it be my time to die, I will die. Nor will I claw at the edges of life, seeking to halt my fall. I have lived long, and the gods have granted me usefulness. I am content.

Sit here by me and lighten my mind with songs and tales, and let me drift as the gods will."

Si-Lun turned away his head that the Seeker might not see his tears. And he sat and talked and sang the afternoon into evening, until the old man slept the deep sleep of fever.

Then, when he was certain that his father-friend would not soon awaken, Si-Lun called the servant to watch over him. He went down from the terrace to the small jetty, where lay the sailing boat belonging to Kla-Noh. As the lights of Shar-Nuhn moved, dancing, across the night-blackened bay, the lean man cast off and loosed the sail to the wind, tacking across the waters, past the bar, into the full tide of the Purple Waters where stood the Tower of Truth.

With great labor, he worked the small vessel near the mighty steps that led from the Tower down into the deeps of the sea. Strongly did the waters move about the Tower, and grim work it was for a man alone to anchor in safety there, but Si-Lun was sailor as well as Seeker, and at length he stood upon the stair and entered the tall door that stood always open.

Twice before had he stood there in the never-wavering light that lit the hall and the stair. Then Kla-Noh had stood beside him, hale and well, and his heart pained him to think of the weakened and wasted man he had become.

In the center of the hall hung a triangular frame strung like a harp with filaments of light. Si-Lun moved forward and ran his fingers lightly across the spectrum within the frame. A deep and musical hum filled the air, seeming to echo from the depths and the heights of the Tower. Then a door opened above, on the spiraling stair, and Ru-Anh, the Father of Initiates, descended, his blue robes moving silently in the warm air.

Si-Lun saluted him and stood waiting for his greeting.

"Well met, my friend Si-Lun," said the Initiate. "Long has it been since our eyes have been gladdened one with the other. Yet I feel that you are come to me in troubled case, and I am here to aid and to advise you."

"It is true," said Si-Lun. "Heavy is my heart and troubled, and sorely do I need healing aid for my friend and father, Kla-Noh. For he has lain in sickness for many days, fevered and listless, dreaming of death.

"Death is no enemy—he has stood at my side more than once and steadied my hand and my heart, ensuring that one refuge was left to me. Yet I cannot feel that the gods have completed the pattern that is the life of Kla-Noh. As he has grown in years he has grown in wisdom and humanity, giving of himself more and more to all who have need. He will not ask for your aid, but I ask it, in my own behalf. I am not yet finished with learning from Kla-Noh, or with aiding him in pursuit of truth."

Ru-Anh laid his hand upon the young man's shoulder. "Do not despair, my friend. I also cannot feel that the days of Kla-Noh are ripe for the harvester. Strange it is that he should drift into death dreams—always has he struggled. Yet he grows older, as do we all. Hard have been the tasks he has performed, and wearing on the body and the spirit. It may be that he has driven himself past his endurance and now his body has thrust the self aside, seeking to renew itself. Let us go to him, that I may see his need and, mayhap, his cure."

Then the two went down to the sailing craft and cast off into the surging waters, making for the distant shore that held the house of Kla-Noh.

With the rising of To-Sen, they anchored below the terrace and went up the stone steps. Only a faint light glowed from the window where Kla-Noh lay, and they could see the faithful Nu-Veh nodding beside the couch.

At the sound of their footsteps the servant raised his head; Si-Lun went to the terrace window, which opened outward, like a door, and gestured for him to be silent. Nu-Veh came to the window and opened the leaves fully outward, and the two men entered quietly.

Ru-Anh moved to the side of the couch and looked down at the old Seeker. Gray was his lined face, and sunken, and his breathing came in shallow gasps. Through his sleep he twitched and frowned, as though troubled by ill dreams. The Initiate looked long, then touched his forehead, moving so slowly and easily that the sleeper did not awaken, but only moaned and sighed. Then Ru-Anh motioned for Si-Lun to retire with him to the sitting room, where they could talk without disturbing their friend.

"He is ill, ill, my friend Kla-Noh, and with sickness of the spirit more than of the body," said the Initiate. "Through my hand I felt the troubled course of his dream, the deeply disturbed pattern of his spirit. Fevered he is, and wasted in body, but such is the result, not the cause, of his unease. To determine this, I must return to the Tower and seek the aid of Nu-Rea, Seeker into the Spirit. Let us go at once, that you may return swiftly here to sustain him with your strength while we probe into his hidden heart."

This was accomplished as speedily as all Si-Lun's skill could achieve it, and within two hours he was again beside the couch of Kla-Noh. Well did he know when the probing mind of Nu-Rea moved within the soul of his friend, for the uneasy sleep of the earlier night deepened into a trancelike state that bore the old man far down into the waters of unconsciousness. Then did Si-Lun reach out his hand and take that of his friend, holding it with all the might of his mind and his body.

Through the parched skin of the old man's hand he could feel a tide of power throbbing and pulsing within that fevered flesh. Dimly he could perceive the working of the mind of the Seeker into the Spirit as she went about her task, and he felt his strength draining into his friend and into that beyond which was working within him. He held himself open to their need, giving all that was in him to give, and as he was absorbed into the quest he began to know and to understand its course and its finding.

When the long ordeal drew to an end, the lean man lay exhausted against the side of the couch, still holding to the hand of Kla-Noh. But Kla-Noh lay in calm and quiet sleep, deep and dreamless, waiting for the dawn.

Then the voice of Ru-Anh spoke in the heart of Si-Lun, saying, "Thus have we determined: the spirit of our friend has gone far down the road to wishful death. The weariness of body, which he seldom admitted even to himself, had grown too great for him to bear. Though he carries himself as one in his prime, yet he is old, and great efforts that we might sustain and recover from in a span of days lie within him as a weight and a heaviness which, at last, have overborne his resolute will.

"We can restore his body, to a degree, but far has his soul moved down that peaceful path, and it is no common healing that can return it to the world of men. He has heard our plea, and yours, and his heart has smiled, but his mind yet moved yonder, toward the waiting door.

"This is his right, yet it is our thought that the world has not done with him. There is need for his singular skills, here and elsewhere. Is there any whose plea might waken him from this walk into the twilight?"

Then Si-Lun sat long and pondered, thinking of all that his friend had told him of his life, and of all that they had done together. At last he said, "Once we two aided one—a lady of great courage and beauty—to deliver herself from a hard usage. Hers was the strength and skill, but it was the wisdom of Kla-Noh that taught her to use them to advantage. We have long wondered as to her fate, for in delivering herself she brought down a great house and the land upon which it stood. There is a way in which I might find if she lives—for if she does live, it is in another order of world than this—and seek her aid or that of her mother, if she lives not.

"They are a people of powers unlike to ours, and it might be that they could find a remedy for the malady of Kla-Noh that is undiscoverable to us. Yet it will require a voyage of some days to come to the place of communication, and a time not to be estimated for communicating and receiving guidance. Can you ease him in his body and restrain him from entering that dim door until my return is accomplished?"

"This we can do," said Ru-Anh. "Go you with all speed, and with our prayers for your success. And to comfort your heart, I will tell you a secret thought that we of the Initiates have had in our minds. It is our intent to ask, one day, that Kla-Noh enter the Tower as one of our order. He has approached the ways of the gods down a different road, but he now draws near to the place of oneness, and we would have him with us."

"Then will I go speedily and return as soon as can be," said Si-Lun.

At once Si-Lun set about preparing for his voyage, outfitting the sloop that was Kla-Noh's vessel for traveling far upon the Purple Waters. Then he slept until the turning of the tide, when he bade farewell to Nu-Veh, looked again upon his sleeping friend, and went forth, setting on all canvas in order to make the most of the fitful wind that still blew from the west.

Southward he sailed, but slowly, cursing the unsteady breezes. But once before had he come this way, and that guided by Kla-Noh, so he attended closely to the shifting of the wind and kept the dim blue line of land upon his starboard, though he knew that it would be long before the rocky cape that he sought would rise from the horizon.

Noon passed into a burning afternoon, and the Purple Waters were like ridged copper, rocked only lightly by the motion of the air. The spinnaker that Si-Lun had hopefully hoisted hung loosely, bellying only occasionally to a puff of wind. The lean man sat by the tiller watching the sky and the sea, but seeing the face of his friend. When night fell, he ate sparingly where he sat. Then he lashed the handle and lay down beside it, disciplining his mind to slumber.

Through the hot night, the sloop moved down the coastline, and only the fitful slatting of the booms and the creaking of the timbers gave notice that she was there, for the moon disappeared, near midnight, behind a wrack of cloud, and before dawn a breeze was making up from the north that sped the vessel upon her way.

Si-Lun was awake with the first gust, and cheerfully did he observe the overcast sky. "Do your worst," he said to the north wind. "You will but send me upon my way, and that is my dearest wish."

Then the north wind blew indeed, as if answering his wish, and the clouds opened, sending blinding rain. But Si-Lun was a son of the sea, and gathering in his spin-

naker, he ran under main and jib sails, flying southward
as a bird to its nest.

No ease did the night bring, and Si-Lun beat seaward,
lest the wind turn and drive him upon the rocky coast.
Long did he reckon upon his progress, calculating
whether he was like to miss the cape in the darkness, but
his reckoning reassured him, and he slept fitfully beneath
reefed sails, feeling with half his senses the condition of
his vessel.

Dawn brought a gray light, ripped with spray, but the
lean man laid on his mainsail and moved toward the
shore. Almost was he even with the cape before he saw it
looming out of the wild wet air. He reefed all sail and
crept into the lee of the stony point, working into the little cove that it sheltered from the north wind. Then did
he go below at last, to dry himself and to prepare hot
food.

Warmed and fed, he rested for a space before returning to the wind-wrapped world above. When he fastened
his carefully prepared pack upon his shoulders, he
counted in his mind the things it contained. The herbs
were there, yes, with a fagot of wood, lest that within the
forest where he went be too wet to burn. There also was
the Shamal of Kla-Noh, that faceted gem of topaz color
which might let him speak with the Initiates, should the
need arise. A little food, dry clothing. Yes, all was there.
He looked about the snug cabin where he and his friend
had made merry on many a voyage. "So shall we again,"
he vowed. Then he went on deck and ashore.

It was not easy to find the steep path that led from the
cove to the high meadows that lay about the head of the
cape, for the wind and the rain moved the young pines
across the narrow trail and whipped their aromatic nee-
dles into his eyes and across his face. Yet he persisted, and

reached the top at last. But when he peered, squinting, into the distance, seeking the outline of the wood that he must reach, it was hidden in the blown mist of clouds that crowned the cape.

Still, he found the line of trees that crossed the meadows, and he followed that, reaching the wood in less time than he had estimated. Little did he think to find the strange stillness that had wrapped that place before, for the wind hissed through the trees and creaked in the branches. Yet once he entered the wood, it enwrapped him in a stillness not of the ear but of the spirit. The trail, which he had walked in darkness but had never seen, went dimly before him, and he followed, feeling his heart grow cool and still within him, and his mind grow bright with a pale light. Then did he stop and open the pack, sheltering the herbs and the fagot until they were twisted into a torch and lit to a goodly blaze. But a few more paces led him to the amphitheater within the trees, circled by standing stones.

Drawing his breath deeply, he walked to the center of the circle and thrust his torch into the riven pillar that stood there. And then the piercing silence that he had fled, once before, descended upon the place, shutting out rain and wind and all thought, save of purpose.

From the air about the pillar came quiet voices. "We are. We have been. We shall be," they whispered. "What need have you?"

Si-Lun sank upon his knees from the weight of the silence, yet his voice was firm as he answered, "Great is my need, O people of another world. Yet must I ask of you, first of all, if there lives among you one called Li-Ah, daughter to your queen. In this world she was and from it she went, but I cannot tell if it was to the realm of her mother or to that of the gods."

There was a storm of whispers, like the humming of a distant hive. Then one voice said, "Li-Ah lives, and is with her mother."

Then the lean man said, "Then know you that Kla-Noh, who aided her in her need, lies at the door to otherwhere, and his spirit seeks to pass. Yet does our world have need of him, and the Initiates, who are those among us closest to the gods, say that they, also, have need of him. Yet so worn is his body with his endeavors in behalf of those in tribulation, his spirit has taken leave of it and will not heed any call for its return, though the Initiates can heal his physical sickness and make him whole again.

"There is none among us who can do more than this. Only one could I recall whose voice might reach him in those dim ways in which he moves, and that is Li-Ah, for he was greatly moved by her beauty and her strength, and she has held a place in his heart since he first beheld her. Her call might turn him from that final door and send him up dreamlike halls again to the land of the living."

"You ask much," the voices crooned. "We are here for the service of those who live . . . elsewhere . . . yet we do not disturb our high ones with the troubles of those distant folk. What token have you that might speak to Li-Ah?"

"Ask her to speak with Si-Lun, in memory of the Cat with the Sapphire Eyes," replied the lean man, shifting wearily upon his aching knees.

Then was there a long silence, as if the voices were taken aback. Then a longer silence, and Si-Lun began to hope. For how long a space he knelt there, held in his trancelike state, he was unable to reckon. Yet there was an answer, at last, in a voice he knew of old.

"Scarcely do I know you, my friend Si-Lun, when you are not crouched beneath a golden-flowered bush. Yet do I know you and have come with all speed to aid you and my wise friend Kla-Noh."

And when Si-Lun had laid before her the matter, the lady considered for a space. Then she said, "Now do I need to look upon the face of Kla-Noh again, and to lay my hand upon his. I must, therefore, return for a time to your world, and this is not a simple thing. To send a voice or a seeing thought, this is matter most simple, but to come through in the flesh requires much. Still, there are ways known to your Initiates, as to our Teachers of Truth. And I feel the presence of an object of power. Is there not in your possession a thing that is of the Initiates?"

Then Si-Lun drew forth the Shamal and set it before him upon the edge of his cloak. But something drew him farther, and he rose and set it upon the top of the pillar that held the burnt-out torch he had placed there. The sunny crystal seemed to draw light from the touch of the stone, and its facets began to glow with supernal fire.

"This is the device that allows us to reach the Tower of Truth, wherever we may be," said Si-Lun.

From the air above the crystal a whisper began to be heard, growing stronger, though no hand was laid upon it to warm it with human strength. Soon it was strongly audible, saying, "We are here. We are here. We are here."

The voice of Li-Ah sounded, near to the gem. "I am Li-Ah, who lives in another place than your world. Your messenger, Si-Lun, has told me of the plight of our friend Kla-Noh, and I would return to your world in order to aid him. You have, I know, the secret of the powered crystal that can move men from place to place upon the planet.

Do you set it in the range above that which you use, and turn your thoughts toward things unknown and unseen. Then will I come into your place."

Ru-Anh's deep voice now sounded from the gem. "This will we do, but there is danger, and we would caution you as to your peril."

"No stranger I to travel by such means," said the lady, laughing. "In three days' time I shall be ready to come. When your sun stands at zenith, then power you your crystal, and I shall appear. With the aid of the gods, we shall warp the stuff of time and matter to work the cure of this Seeker."

Si-Lun seemed to awaken slowly from a dream. The Shamal lay upon the pillar, its fiery glow quieted to a glimmer. The voices were stilled, and the silence had lifted from the spot, leaving wind rush and rainfall to speak alone. The Seeker gathered his pack together and stood, feeling a long ache in his bones and stiff crickles in his muscles. But he hurried from the place as swiftly as he could move, spurred by the need to return to Shar-Nuhn with all speed.

Now the wind no longer sang fiercely from the north, though the rain fell in long sheets across the waters. Si-Lun was able to tack close to the wind, and he blessed the fleet sloop as he worked her ever nearer to his destination.

Before dawn on the third day, in the light breeze from the east that had followed upon the track of the northerly storm, the lean man saw the lights of Shar-Nuhn rise from the waters before him. Then did he make his thanks to the gods.

Straight to the waters near the Tower did he go, and anchored to the leeward, taking his small boat to approach the steps. At the doorway he was met by Ru-Anh, who greeted him with pleasure and urged him to eat and to rest himself.

"Soon enough will I do both, O Father of Initiates," said Si-Lun, "but first I must know how fares my father and friend. Lingers he still this side of the dark doorway?"

"His body rests and heals itself," said Ru-Anh. "His spirit still wanders in dimness, seeking to draw nigh to that way which leads into death. Yet have we held him in our tenderest snares, holding him from his way as one holds the questing child from the hearthfire."

"Then will I rest and make ready for Li-Ah," said the Seeker.

Long before noon, however, the lean man was about the Tower, waiting impatiently for the Initiates to summon him to the chamber of the crystal. Slowly did the time wheel move, but at length the chime of noon rang, and those concerned were gathered in the round chamber, gazing into the curving alcove that held the gently shimmering blue of the crystal.

When the rods and the pulsing knobs were set as Li-Ah had instructed, all stood in concentration, sending their spirits along the strange track that she must travel. As they stood thus, the ridged half-sphere that was the crystal pulsed into azure ripples, and sparks of light began to move within its depths, giving the impression of infinite motion, infinite speed.

Still the Initiates concentrated, but Si-Lun, unlearned in the ways of mind-sending, watched the alcove in fascination, seeing the outlines of the chair within its cup grow blurred, as if it were vibrating to strange rhythms. Then, as though a shadow were congealing, a shape began to grow. Glints of rich green flickered in the chair, a shimmer of chestnut hair, a flash of smoke-blue eyes, and there sat the ghost of Li-Ah, growing more real, more solid, as each instant passed.

Then, as one, the Initiates opened their eyes, and Ru-Anh turned to his panel of instruments. The glow in the crystal died again to a gentle shimmer, and the lights ceased to flicker within it.

Li-Ah stood, and all made obeisance to her, so royal was her presence. She smiled upon all, then turned to Ru-Anh. "My greetings, Wise One," she said. "Well have you wrought with us in this. My mother, La-Shia, sends also her well-wishes. She has promised to follow our endeavors with her seeing thought, and to aid us, should there be need."

She took the hand of Si-Lun, who had approached shyly as a child, abashed by her presence. "My friend, we shall go now to look upon Kla-Noh. And when we have worked for him as we may, we might return, might we not, to have long talk with these Wise Ones of your world? Much have we, my mother and I, to tell and to ask them."

Then the two, with Ru-Anh following behind, went down through the Tower and out to the sloop and away across the waters to Kla-Noh, who still waited in his silken slumber for the dawn that they brought to him in the light of their faces and the power of their spirits and their hands.

XI

The Shadow That Swallowed the World

A fresh breeze from the east crisped the Purple Waters into ripples that the morning sun trimmed with gilded crests. Upon the terrace of Kla-Noh sat the Seeker with Si-Lun and Li-Ah, their guest this fortnight.

The old Seeker lay in a low chair, shaded from the fullness of the sun, and his face was marked with the traces of recent illness. He gazed with the childish interest of the convalescent alternately at his foster son and the lady as they bantered, one with the other. Much pleasure did their friendship give the old man, and he smiled at their eager faces more often than at their words.

Out of the indistinct line of the horizon, far across the waters, moved a cloud, sweeping its grape-tinted shadow across the glinting wave tops. There came a pause in the lighthearted chatter, and Si-Lun watched as the spot of moving darkness approached, crossed the bay, and moved inland. A sudden sadness appeared upon his face, as if something had wrenched at his heart, and his companions sensed that his light mood was banished in the short span of a flying cloud.

"Once," said the lean man, "I saw such a cloud. And when it moved past my world, there was no longer a world for me."

Li-Ah laid her hand lightly upon his, and Kla-Noh nodded. "It can be," the old Seeker said softly, "that even in the short interval of a heartbeat what has been utter reality can become insubstantial as the ghost of a dream."

"Aye," breathed Si-Lun. "So it was with me. Would you hear the tale?"

"Yes," they answered, and thus he began:

* * *

From my earliest years, I was called by the sea. Though my father apprenticed me early to a wicked master, I was able to free myself and, with the help of the Initiates of my own land, I went to sea in an honest ship, under a fair captain. Clean was the life, and hard and strongly disciplined, but such was my nature that I was uplifted by it, and did not grow surly and brutal, as some do. The sea was my joy and my work and all the life I wanted, and I labored at my tasks.

Before I was possessed of twenty summers, I was overseer of the deck crews, aboard the *Lu-La*, and in two more seasons I was chosen by the master as his lesser officer. There was some grumbling among the seamen, because of my youth, but all knew my labors and my studies, and none openly opposed me. So I gloried in duties and felt that never would I have need of further joy than I possessed.

The continent of my birth is vast, with shorelines upon two oceans. But trade is carried on across the Purple Waters from many ports along the hither coast. And it is true, though few have proven the way, that the great land bridge upon which Shar-Nuhn is placed is backed, far in the west, by another ocean, studded with populous islands and rimmed with prosperous cities.

Yet in order to reach this ocean, it is necessary to beat far to the southward along coasts that grow increasingly steep and forbidding, avoiding shoal waters that extend far out to sea, and tacking against adverse winds that blow out of the southern waters. So time-consuming a voyage is no profitable thing for a merchantman, and few have ever made the attempt twice.

The ship upon which I sailed was owned by adventuresome traders, anxious for exotic goods to stock their shops, which catered to the trade of the wealthy and noble. So great was the profit to be made upon such a cargo that it well repaid the long and hazardous voyage. So we were sent, in our turn, upon the track of their fleet, which regularly went into the Third Ocean to trade for their precious stuffs.

Of the voyage I can say little, save that we learned each of the hazards by heart, through repetition, and our patience wore thin as our waists with turning out in darkness to trim sail in order to avoid reefs and shoals and standing rocks that thrust quite aimlessly from a clear sea. But we cleared the land at last, and made our westering, to come around into the far waters.

Then did our perils seem to be over, and we lazed in warm winds and fished from the end of the swaying boom, what time our duties did not send us scrubbing and mending and making sail. And in the midst of our ease, a terrible wind came upon us, hurling us with incredible swiftness into waters where none of our number had ever been before.

For nights and days that we were too wearied to count, we were tossed and flung and thrust as a chip on the brook, and when at last we heard the shrilling of the wind slacken and felt the seas abate, we found ourselves in a sea where the sun hung far in the northern sky. Night brought formations of stars that none could name, save for some old friends that hung deep in the north.

Then did we take counsel, the captain, his elder officer,

and I, to determine what seemed best to do. All agreed, after some wild speculation, that we must simply steer northward, following our lodestone's pointing finger, until we came to some inhabited land where we could take bearings. And this we did, though when we sighted the sun through our instruments we found ourselves far to the west of our intended destination. We bore north by east and made fair headway through the blood-warm waters that washed in gray-green sluggishness about our hull.

For weary days we moved back upon the track that we had traveled so swiftly when borne upon the storm. Water grew low in the barrels, and our food was limited, for we had never intended to run far from coastlines where all could be replenished at need. So it was with relief that we sighted a conical mountain, seeming to rise alone from the sea. As we drew nearer, we could see that it was set in the midst of a green peninsula, which was in turn connected by a curving link to a wide land beyond.

In the curve of the harbor formed by the mainland and the land link there was a town, whose bustle of vessels, small and large, in and out of the anchorage betokened a busy trading center. Then did the captain knit his brows and set upon his face his dickering look, for well did he know that he might find, in this unknown place, goods that could enrich his masters and himself because of their strangeness.

We anchored well off and went ashore in a small boat to arrange for a berth and whatever permits and assurances these people required of trading vessels. The captain left the Elder to oversee the welfare of the ship, and he took me with him, with four seamen to handle the boat. We had made fast to the wharf, and I had reached to take the captain's chart case from his lifted hand when

I felt a terrific blow upon my head and blackness descended as if the sky had gone out like to a blown candle.

When I woke, it was dark, and I lay for a time trying to remember what had happened to bring me to a bed clothed with smooth draperies, in a room that was faintly scented with a flower perfume I could not identify. At last I felt equal to the effort of raising my hand to my face, when I discovered the cause of the darkness. My entire head was swathed in bandages, which covered my eyes and even the bridge of my nose.

Then a hand was laid cautioningly upon my own and a voice said firmly, "You must not disarrange the bandages." It required a time for me to puzzle out the words, for they were spoken in the language of Shar-Nuhn, which I had learned well, but with a strange twist to the accent. Nonetheless I lowered my hand and asked, "Where is my captain?"

The voice replied, "He is with my father, who is harbor master in Noroven."

"And how came I here, with swathings round my uneasy head?" I asked.

Then she laughed, and I discovered that none I had ever known had understood the art. "You were struck," said she, "by a great basket of flounder, swinging up and out of the hold of a fisher vessel. The catcher upon the wharf chose that moment to sneeze mightily, with the result that he missed the basket, which caught you well and truly. Much was the uproar, for you went forward over your own boat into the harbor, and all were frantically fishing and paddling about in search of you.

"It may amuse you to know that it was your captain who saw you at last, and he asked none other but dived in himself to pull you from the water. One may easily see that he thinks well of you, for he would not dry himself until he had seen you well attended, safe in my father's own house."

Then I laughed also, though sorely did it hurt my head.

For three days I lay in the harbor master's house, and Ni-Sha, his daughter, cared for me in most sisterly fashion. My captain visited me each day, and well was he pleased with his trading with the merchants of Noroven, for he was finding rare stuffs and strange artifacts enough to make his whole cargo, so that he could sail at once for home when all was arranged.

On the third day after my accident, the physician (for there they had no Initiates) came at his accustomed time, and I prevailed upon him to let me rise from the bed, so that I could begin to regain my strength. He was reluctant, but agreed at last, and I took his arm and rose to my feet.

To my dismay, I found that as soon as I sought to stand erect, my head spun with terrible swings, and nausea gripped my throat. Only when I again lay flat did the turmoil cease, though I lay gasping for a time thereafter.

"Heavy blows to the head," the physician told me, "can cause such distress for some time. We shall seek to raise you higher each day, by means of pillows, until you are used to the upright position once again. Then we shall see."

When the captain came that afternoon, I sought to have him return me to the ship, for I felt that my presence, in such a condition, could only be a burden upon my patient hosts. But he told me that the physician had cautioned him against such a move, as it might complicate my recovery. And Ni-Sha and her father protested against it so sincerely that I no longer felt myself to be an embarrassment to them.

Now the time grew short, for the cargo was purchased

and all but loaded into the holds. Each day I strove to sit, to stand, but the implacable vertigo was always there. Then did I speak with my captain and with the physician. And both said the same.

"Si-Lun," said the captain, "it is sore telling, yet tell I must. You cannot sail with us on this voyage. The physician affirms that the motion of the vessel, even should you be able to stand or sit, would give you agony, and the nausea would melt the flesh from your bones long before we could reach the home port. You must stay in Noroven until next a vessel of our fleet seeks it out, and that will be but a year or two, for our owners will find ready market for the things that can be found here.

"Nay, do not fret." He smiled, pushing me back upon the couch. "I have found use for you, even here. The good harbor master has rented me this room for your use, and all is paid in full. You will be able more and more to care for yourself, and in a month or so, the physician assures me, you will be yourself, so long as you keep to the steady earth. Then may you go to work for the harbor master, aiding him in his dealings with vessels from afar, for you have learned many strange dialects in your associations with seafarers upon the Purple Waters. And, as you have opportunity, you may discover unusual goods such as our owners covet. Then you may draw upon the account that I have made with our friend and purchase what you consider a bargain, and store your goods in one of the warehouses. Thus, when one of our fleet enters the harbor, the work is done, and all the master need do is to load the cargo and set sail. You will act as our agent, as well as the assistant to the harbor master. What say you?"

Then I thought of the delight of remaining within the sound of Ni-Sha's laugh, with useful work and a whole unseen land to wander in, while I waited.

"You have provided for me as a son," I told the captain. "And I shall be happy in the work you have given me. My thanks to you for your concern."

So when the *Lu-La* moved away upon the tide, I was not desolate, though lonely it was to see her go, leaving none in the whole of Noroven who had ever seen the Purple Waters, save a solitary lad called Si-Lun.

Long weeks went by before I could well stand and walk, and even then I must guard against sudden turnings or motions of the head. Yet mend I did, as youth will, and before two months had passed I was able to take my place in the chambers of the harbor master. There I found much to interest me and to keep me busy, for I determined to master the language of Noroven and, with the help of Ni-Sha and her father, this I soon did. Then could I truly aid in the work of the port, checking the listings of the wharfage and the cargo manifestos of the vessels which flocked there. Soon the harbor master entrusted his accounts to me, and long would I sit in the evening over the spidery columns of figures.

But all was not labor. Many were the days of celebration upon the land of Noroven, when the merchants closed their shops and the people who lived inland came to the port in decorated carts to rejoice in their temples and to dance the nights through in the grassy parks that studded the city. On those days, Ni-Sha would put a bottle of wine and a selection of fruit, a bit of cheese, and her good brown bread into a basket, and we would run away, we two, into the wooded hills upon the mainland, riding long-legged beasts that she would borrow from her grandmother, a craggy old lady who lived at the edge of the farmland.

Upon the crest of one of the hills we would dismount and eat ravenously, as all younglings do, I suppose. Then we would nap in the long grass, to wake with crickets in our hair and down our necks. Afterward we would ramble on foot through the forests, chattering fit to silence the birds. We would return to the city, brown and merry and ravenous again, and the harbor master would chuckle roundly as we recounted our tremendous discoveries, while we consumed platesful of his good food.

For a year we lived thus, and I grew to feel as much one of the family as though I had been born the harbor master's son. But one day I realized that I did not care to become Ni-Sha's brother. Then did I go straightaway to her father and told him how I felt, and that I sought to wed her.

Then his sharp blue eyes twinkled at me wickedly as he said, "Well then, my son, do you court her as you would charm a little squirrel from a tree, never letting her see your purpose. With patience, you may change her feeling for you to that of a sweetheart. Though with a hoyden like my daughter it will be a mighty task, for she ever bore herself as though she were a son to me, and no daughter. Yet you may succeed, and then you would be my son indeed, and that would please me truly."

So I set about courting Ni-Sha. Not with flowers and pretty sayings and simperings in secret. Those things she laughed to scorn. But I talked with her of dreams and aspirations, of things past and of things that might be. I endeavored to show to her the working of my spirit, that she might know if it were one she could love. As time went by, she seemed, more and more, to think of me as one to consult in perplexity, to rely upon in adversity.

The day came when I asked her to wed, and her answer pleased both me and her father. The rites in their temple were simple and grave, and they left us with quiet joy in our hearts. Our love was as sweet as our friendship had been, and still it was spiced with our old teasing and talking. Then we were indeed as a family should always be. Her father grew daily more round and cheerful, and we moved as lengths of light about the wharves and the warehouses, working in a haze of happiness.

In the midst of the second spring of my stay in Noroven, my lady came to me with a grave face, from which a smile was attempting to slip at the corner of her dimpled mouth.

"My lord," said she (which she always did when teasing), "you must comport yourself with more dignity in future. A father must be a model of decorum."

Then was I lost in bliss, dreaming of the future while enjoying the present fully. The months slipped away in a bustle of planning and anticipation. At midwinter we found ourselves the possessors of a small male being with a mighty voice and a noticing eye. All promptly succumbed to his power, and he ruled the house.

As the spring wore into summer, my father-in-love began to wear an expression of greater-than-normal smugness. Often would he absent himself in the evenings, returning well after his grandson's bedtime, which deprived him of his usual playtime with the child. Ni-Sha and I well knew that he plotted some surprising thing for us, so we were suspiciously unsuspicious, that we might not spoil his plan.

One evening, when the slanting sunlight bathed the port in honey and balm, he suggested that we take a short drive in the pony cart, following the curve of the harbor onto the peninsula, whose thick woods and trimmed fields beckoned with green-gold enticements. We quickly completed the tasks of the day, stored in the cart spare sail for our young mariner, and were away quickly. Joyful was the lap of the waters to our right, the green of the tended orchards and gardens to our left, as we clipped along.

The mountain that crowned the peninsula rose fair before us as the road swung inland, and we began to enter the fringes of the woods that cloaked it. Strange was the shape of that peak, and I said to Ni-Sha's father, "Yonder is an unusual shape for a mountain. I was reared among towering crags, all worn into crevices and showing their underpinning rock. Yet that is unlike those that I know, for it is so symmetrical a cone that one would think it hewn by the hand of man."

"There are others to match it, far inland to the west," answered my father-in-love. "There are tales the old ones tell to frighten the younglings concerning that prominence. Wild tales, mostly, of the earth shaking and smoke and flame gushing from the top and the sides, as if it were a dragon or a blacksmith's forge! Nonsense, all agree who are practical men. Nonetheless, it is a queer one, right enough."

Our way now wound up around the hills that circled the mountain's foot, and our eyes delighted in the changing perspectives and unexpected views. Now and again we would pass a villa belonging to one of the well-to-do merchants in Noroven, or a well-groomed farm with its apron of green and its background of vineyard and orchard and tree-studded meadows. Ni-Sha looked with joy upon them, saying, "Since I was little older than our manling here, I wished to live upon these slopes, amid the green of the trees. One day, perhaps, we may find it possible."

Truly, I agreed, it would be the perfect place for bringing up our children. Then we rounded a gentle curve in the twisting road, and there stood a house—not overly large, but capacious—to which our father pointed with high good humor.

"One day, indeed!" said he. "Now, if you please. I cannot have my grandson pining away in the noise and jostle of the town. Here there is room for him to chase butterflies and wade in the brook that flows yonder, and wander the mountainside unhindered. For I have purchased yon villa, subject only to your approval, for my marriage gift to you."

The innocent joy in his blue eyes stifled any twinge of unease I had at accepting so great a gift, and Ni-Sha turned to him a face so full of pleasure that it must have been reward enough in itself. Even little Lu-Sta lay crowing in his basket as though he knew that his elders were happy.

Then did we get down from the cart and wander, making sounds of delight at everything. The house was trim and snug. The gardens waited only for a guiding hand to burst into fruit and flower. A neat byre was concealed by the orchard plot, with room for a milk cow and riding beasts, and a serenely chuckling brook wound through all.

"Surely, father Sta-Ni, none ever made a gift that was more delighted in," I said to him when all had been examined and admired. "Here will we live in joy and bring up many grandchildren for your delight."

Thus it was. We found it a haven of happiness. My short journey into the town each day was no burden, and the return in the evening to my waiting family was a small adventure every time. When next a ship of our fleet anchored in the harbor, I hailed it with joy, but never thought of returning in her to my other life. Her captain was well pleased with the store of goods that I had garnered without haste, seeking out good values, exotic stuffs, at fair prices. So when I told him that, if he was willing to continue the system begun by my captain, I should remain in Noroven as agent for our owners and aide to the harbor master, he agreed and renewed the account, that I might purchase more for the next ship to make landfall there.

Another son came to us after a time, and a dark-haired hoyden who vied with her brothers even in the cradle. Their grandfather was their fastest friend, and three evenings of five he made the short journey to our door to eat the evening meal with us and to have a fair frolic with the younglings afterward. Never will my memory relinquish the sight of his portly figure upended upon the rug, robe tails about his ears and pens falling like rain, as he taught them to stand on their heads.

As I recall that time, it seems that it must have been in another world, another universe. Such happiness comes seldom to humankind, and for it the gods exact payment.

There came a day of golden sun and blue sky, like many others in Noroven. From my place of work I would look, when the opportunity came, at the mountain across the bay, thinking of my home upon the slopes. Much cargo was there in the warehouses, newly purchased, and for some hours I was busied in their dark caverns, counting and valuing. When next I emerged into the day, I was astonished to see the streets full of people, who were staring in wonderment at the mountain. Then did I run also into the street and turn my gaze there.

Beneath my feet I could feel a strange growling in the earth, as if it groaned in its depths. The bay slopped about as if it were a carelessly held bowl of water, but the mountain—oh, the mountain! From its top there spread a haze of shadow, darker than cloud, and in its side I could see a rift that opened farther as I watched. Then there burst forth a dreadful pall of inky blackness that spread down the side of the peak in a rush. Before my eyes it moved across the spot where I knew my world was centered. Down it rushed toward Noroven, and I wished it to hurry, for my heart knew that it bore death.

Then a breeze sprang forth from the mainland, driving the darkness away at an angle, across the bay and out to sea. Upon the slopes there was stillness, and I moved with hopeless speed to secure my riding beast. As I mounted, Sta-Ni appeared in the stable door.

"Go with all speed," he cried to me. "I shall follow as quickly as I may upon my slow beast. Go you, with my prayers."

But there was none left to succor when I arrived.

Thus it was that my world ended, upon a fair afternoon beneath a sky of perfect peace.

I moved myself into the house of Sta-Ni, and we two drifted about it as two ghosts about a tomb. The business went on its usual way, and we attended blindly, yet our hearts were dead within us and we went for days without speaking, save by necessity.

Sta-Ni lived a month. It is not easy for a man in good health to die of his own will, without raising his hand against himself, but I saw him dying and I could not bring myself to deter him. No physician did I call, though I tended him lovingly as I could. But well did I wish that I could do the same, and I would not delay him from his journey.

When next a vessel of the fleet anchored in Noroven, I gave the house to the people of the temple, to administer for the good of those in need, in the name of Sta-Ni and those he loved. Then I boarded the ship, and we sailed away from Noroven upon a fair wind, and little did the crew or the captain know that they bore a ghost among their living complement.

XII

The Terror from the Hills

A miasma of uneasiness crept about Shar-Nuhn. In the Tower, the Initiates felt a nameless chill in their spirits. About the warehouses of the merchants, the taverns at wharfside, the homes of the commonplace, and the great houses of the wealthy there was a wary watchfulness, without cause or reason that any could name.

In the house of Kla-Noh there was gloom, but for long the old Seeker attributed it to the loneliness he and Si-Lun felt after their guest had left. Si-Lun was glum and silent, and Kla-Noh felt like a cat whose fur is stroked backward, ready to hiss and claw. But time went by, and neither grew more cheerful. Then did the Seeker begin to seek into causes.

Sailing across the bay, he nosed about the wharves and tasted wine in the taverns, listening, listening all the while. In the air over Shar-Nuhn he seemed to feel a tension that teased the skin as would a thousand invisible spider webs. And the people were irritable. Old acquaintances took offense at casual inquiries. Shipmates fought blindly in the taverns at night, sometimes drawing blood. The merchants were barely civil to their wealthiest customers, and no more serious signal of malaise had Kla-Noh ever encountered. But the old man said nothing, merely nodded wisely into his wine cup, and observed.

He roused the lethargic Si-Lun, who seemed lost in a tragic dream, and went out into the Purple Waters where the Tower reared its shining column. But the Initiates had no clue. All their skills had they exerted to find the root of the problem. Nu-Rea, the Seeker into the Spirit, lay in exhaustion, having sent her spirit abroad in all directions, seeking the source, until her strength was dissipated.

Ru-Anh was distraught, a condition in which none had ever seen the Father of Initiates in all memory. Some of the Initiates were ill in body, all were disturbed in spirit, and no help was to be found in the Tower of Truth, which was the sole source in Shar-Nuhn of healing and teaching, of aid and comfort.

Then did Si-Lun waken somewhat from his grim mood. In shocked speculation, he rowed his foster father from the Tower to their craft; and when they were set for their anchorage below the terrace, he said, "Surely, my friend, this is some enchantment of terrible power, for none has ever affected the Initiates in all of time."

Then Kla-Noh shook himself as if emerging from deep thought and replied, "Some such it may be. Yet enchantment is a weak thing, dealing with powers that cannot create the real, only the illusion. I have a strange feeling concerning this malady. My bones tell me, my nose tells me, all my instincts tell me . . ." But here he trailed into silence and would say no more.

When they arrived at their anchorage, he hurried at once to his dovecote under the roof. From marked cages he took special birds and attached messages to their red legs, then cast them free into the air. Then he schooled

himself to wait in patience for the return of his own
birds, which those whom he contacted held for reply.

Long days went by, and none in Shar-Nuhn found
ease. The very animals in the stables and the byres upon
outlying farms were affected, as Kla-Noh found upon in-
vestigation. He wandered afar, with Si-Lun at his side,
watching, listening, thinking deeply all the while. He
found that the wild birds were forsaking their rookeries
along the shores of the Purple Waters. The chipmunks in
the farm walls and the mice in the granaries were nerv-
ous past their natural wont. No living thing, save only the
insects, walked in its old way about its business.

Then the pigeons began to return to the cote. Kla-Noh
welcomed them with joy and began at once deciphering
messages, day by day as they arrived. From the south
they came, but their far-borne answers gave no aid. From
the west, across the poisoned barrens, they came, and
none there knew what Kla-Noh needed to know. None
came from the east, for the Purple Waters lay in rolling
vastness there. But from the north there came word that
brought light to the Seeker's eyes and hope to his voice.

He called Si-Lun from the terrace into the sitting room,
where he unrolled maps upon the reading table and lit
the lamp to aid their sight, though day still warmed the
sky. "To the north of Shar-Nuhn," he began, "lie hills.
Low in the beginning, but they become larger, rounder,
steeper, the farther one travels. As a sailor, you would not
have become familiar with that country, for no cities nor
ports are there, only the hills, tenanted by beasts and
birds and an occasional farmer who values his solitude.

"And by a hermit who went there from Shar-Nuhn in
order to study the stars from the eminence of those hills,
unimpeded by lights of men. Him do I know and respect,
and from him I have received word. In the hills there is

terror—far worse than the unease of this city, from his description. The animals cower in their coverts and the farmers barricade their houses. No thing can be seen or heard, but all walk in fear from day's end to day's end. Though he is a learned man of quiet mind, he also is afraid, but he cannot say of what he is terrified.

"Seeking for the source of his unease, he walked northward and found that the terror grew more appalling the farther he ventured. At last the blackness grew to be more than he could bear, and he returned to his hilltop, to find my messenger waiting there. He begs for aid, for life is an ill burden beneath such a weight."

"Then we shall surely aid him—and all who suffer beneath this evil," said Si-Lun, his green eyes beginning to glow with their old fire. "Where a timid hermit might find his limbs failing him, two stalwart Seekers may walk without hindrance."

Then did Kla-Noh place his hand upon the shoulder of the young man. "For such reasons as this, I know you for the son of my spirit," he said. "Truly have you spoken. We shall go, we two, into the hills, taking no riding beasts, for their fear would impede our journey. Upon our feet, bearing our packs upon our backs and the work of the gods within our hearts, we shall walk into the lands where terror reigns.

"And though the Initiates are weakened, nonetheless we shall take with us the Shamal, so that we may communicate with them through the gem, should need arise. For I have a feeling in my innermost being . . ." And again his voice whispered into silence.

With the aid of Nu-Veh, the little servant, they packed thriftily the things they would need. Often as they worked, Si-Lun looked anxiously at his foster father, seeking signs of his recent illness, yet the old man seemed again hale and well, and the vigor of his purpose infused him with strength. Soon they were prepared, and after a night's rest they set forth in the small sailing craft for a safe anchorage that Kla-Noh knew in the northern waters, at the foot of the hill country.

Upon the morning of their second day from home they were ready to set out into the hills, leaving their craft tethered snugly to await their return. The warm colors of fall now lay upon the patches of wood that studded the rolling country, and the sunny day should have made that trek a cheerful thing. But no cheer was there in all the land. A gloom not of the eye enwrapped all who drew breath and possessed warm blood. Each step seemed to sink into quagmire, and each breath caught in the throat. The Seekers, knowing that the malaise would grow far worse, trudged on without comment, working their way deeper into the hills, which climbed ever more steeply about their path.

Their camp that night was a thing to be forgotten quickly. The lengthening shadows crawled with nameless dread, and later the firelight peopled the darkness with shadows out of nightmare. They huddled together in their blankets, finding what comfort they could from the touch of their shoulders and the sounds of their breathing. There were few night sounds. A silence brooded over the hills unbroken by the scuttling of the small creatures that should have ventured out into the night in search of food. No rodent scurried past, no distant howl marked a hunting wolf, no owl whispered across the hard and star-studded sky. Sleep was nothing to seek in that night, so they dozed and waked, dozed and waked, resting their bodies as best they might.

Yet dawn brought little respite. Only their resoluteness of spirit moved them forward into that terrible country in the teeth of the mindless impulse to flee that gripped them by their throats.

At midday they reached the house of the hermit Go-Shu, and his welcome was heartfelt. Though he was a man in late middle years, the past weeks had worn away his face into lines of agony and his hair was whitening. He hurried down the path toward them as they toiled up his steep hill, and they could hear his voice long before they could distinguish his words. Well pleased were they to enter a door and to sit within four walls again. Hot food and long talk cheered them greatly, heartening them for the difficult journey that yet lay before them.

"Not for long has my house been so full of comfort," said the hermit, when they were settled by his hearthfire. "Fear has filled it to the brim these days, as a cup with water. My lone spirit has cowered here, fearful of staying, powerless to leave. Your bird bore upon its leg more comfort than you thought to send with your message."

"Your message brought to me more hope than you knew," replied Kla-Noh. "For this malaise is widespread, embracing Shar-Nuhn and all its inhabitants. Because of your reply, I knew in which direction to search for the cause, and your description of the conditions here gave me an idea—not more than that—of what sort of thing the cause might be."

Then both Si-Lun and the hermit importuned him, but the old Seeker only shook his head and said, "A suspicion is not a fact. The fact we must hunt out and examine in the strong light of reason. Then we will know."

They slept, that night. Though the creeping fear seeped through the walls of the house, they did not feel the terrible insecurity of their night in the open, and their weariness served them well. But morning found them grimly preparing to set out again into the haunted hills.

To their surprise, Go-Shu asked to go with them. "It is no man's part to cower within walls when others go out to do work that I should also be doing. Alone, I was at the mercy of the terror in the countryside, but with two companions such as yourselves I will go back. Now I may control my cowardly limbs, with you to shore me up, and mayhap I shall be of use in this dreadful task."

"Then we shall welcome you, for a wise man is always a good companion and ally," said Si-Lun, and Kla-Noh smiled.

"Now do you sound like my friend Go-Shu. Come and welcome. Let us be off," he said.

Then did they take the road again, moving from paths to tracks, and from tracks into wilds that had not known the foot of man for many years. And as they moved, so did the fear grow in intensity, until only their stout spirits and the fellowship of their comrades bolstered their spirits and strengthened their limbs.

They saw few animals, fewer birds. The small creatures seemed to have left the tainted lands. Once, deep in the night, they heard the far howl of a wolf, just on the edge of hearing. It seemed to be the voice of all the fears that focused on the place, keening through the darkness. Then the three gripped hands round their little fire and drew strength from one another.

There came a day when it seemed more than flesh could accomplish to set foot before foot. Their breath seemed frozen in their gelid lungs, and the muscles of their breasts seemed locked in suffocating bands. Then did Kla-Noh stop and gaze intently toward a tree-cloaked hill that rose just to the north of their path.

"There," he whispered. "There is the source. I feel it, I smell it, I know it in my bones. On the bluff atop that hill, hidden by those twisted oaks, bides the source of this awful mystery. Is there strength in our bodies yet to climb this slope? Can we, when it is climbed, hope to accomplish what we came to do?" And the old man fell silent, staring into the tree shadow, shivering in the sunlight.

Then Si-Lun stepped forward to his side. "Aye," he said. "We can do what is needful, whatever comes. Let us leave our packs here, that we may climb more easily. Give me your arm, and I will lend you my vigor." And he took the old man's arm and held his other hand to Go-Shu, who clasped it tightly. Then all three moved up together, chilled in the strong light of day by the waves of terror which washed that sunlit slope.

Upon the crest of the hill there was a little clearing in the oaks, about the rocky bluff that rose steeply. Amid the crevices in the face of the bluff the approaching men could see a dark cranny that seemed to run back into the hillside. Before this Kla-Noh stopped, head drooping, panting with the effort of self-mastery.

"Within this place," he said, "is the fountain from which the terror flows. Si-Lun, my son-in-faith, bear me up that I may have strength to enter."

Si-Lun squeezed his arm, and Go-Shu moved to the other side and caught the old Seeker by the hand. The three worked their way into the crack, without loosing grip upon one another, for the fear beat out from that place like the cold tide of air that blows from an iceberg in the northern seas.

The entrance extended crookedly into the rock wall for some feet, then widened into a fair-sized chamber. This sandy-floored room was lit, dimly, by a torch of twisted fagots, which was thrust into the loose earth underfoot. At the back lay a bundle of something that had vaguely human shape. But facing the entrance, eyes wide with panic, back braced against the wall, hands clenched in its ragged robe, sat a child. A dark bush of hair topped his dirt-smeared face, and clean tracks marked the course of many past tears down the thin cheeks. No sound came from the little being, only a soft hiccupping burble, like a small pot boiling. From him came that veritable wall of cold terror. Before the blast of new emotion released by their appearance the three men went down like reeds before the wind. They lay, gripping hands, faces burrowed into the sand, enduring a hurricane of force that prickled the hair upon their heads and crimped their skin into gooseflesh.

Si-Lun moved at last, loosing his hand from that of Kla-Noh. Rising into a half-crawl, he inched forward against the flow, toward the youngling who sat before him. No sound could he force from his constricted throat, but he tried to smile as he went. Reaching the child, he collapsed for a time into the dust again. When he had rested for a few moments, he thrust himself up onto his hands and looked full into the little face. The eyes were locked into their frozen fear, as if they saw nothing before them. Si-Lun gently raised the edge of the robe that wrapped the little one's legs, and covered his face.

The terror was damped as if a thin door had been closed against a gale. The two by the entrance sat up slowly and began to move toward that other figure within the cave. Stooping over the recumbent form, Kla-Noh drew back the coverings and touched forehead and throat and wrist.

"This woman is far along the road that leads to darkness," he whispered. "She is fevered and starved, I should think, and worn to exhaustion. Do you, Si-Lun, get our packs and you, Go-Shu, find wood among the oak trees and make up a fire. We shall make a strong broth for her, and I have other things that may aid her. Hurry!"

The two sped as he asked, and soon a cookpot from Go-Shu's pack was bubbling on the fire he built, simmering dried meat into thick soup for the woman, who had not moved or opened her eyes. The smell of the food seemed to penetrate the senses of the child at last. He stirred beneath his covering robe, and the aura of fear that still haunted the cavern grew less intense.

Then Kla-Noh left the woman and went to the child. Sitting upon the floor beside him, he lifted the robe from his face and laid his hand upon the forehead. A little, the fixed eyes flickered. The small face wrinkled with effort, and the mouth almost moved. Kla-Noh reached into the neck of his robe and drew forth the Shamal, which he held between his palms for a moment, warming it. The topaz color waxed into flame, and the old Seeker held the crystal before the eyes of the boy, stroking his forehead as he did so. The eyes, which they could now see were a strange shade of aquamarine, seemed drawn to the gem. And when the faraway voices in the stone began to whisper, "We are here. We are here. We are here," a puzzled look came into those tortured orbs. They turned, almost stiffly, in their sockets to gaze up at the face of Kla-Noh, who sat serenely beneath the gaze.

Two large tears rolled down the face, making new marks in the dirt. The Shamal flickered, and the boy turned his eyes back to it, gazed deeply, seemed to sink into relaxation, dreaming into those lambent fires.

Now the voices grew stronger, as Si-Lun drew near and took Kla-Noh's hand. Drawing power from their bodies, the gem burned more and more brightly, and the voices came clearly. "I am here," said the voice of Ru-Anh. "My friend Kla-Noh, where are you? Well do we know that you have sought out and found the source of our incapacity, for our unease has all but left us. Now do we seek to aid you, should you need it."

Kla-Noh sighed, then spoke into the stone. "When I found that all in Shar-Nuhn were wrapped in dread, then did I seek afar to find a direction from which the malaise came. Go-Shu, whom you know, answered one of my messages with a plea of his own. Then I knew where to seek, and Si-Lun and I came at once. Even then, I thought that I might know the source of the fear, for among the secrets in which I used to deal was one I learned in the Far Islands. There a family lived who had a terrible gift of mind-send. When fully grown, and trained in use and control, they were valuable citizens of their land, but one of their infants might terrorize a whole archipelago when it woke in the night from an ill dream. They moved far away to an isolated island, in order to spare their neighbors terror. These unfortunate folk must be of that blood, for the child, who possesses no more than nine or ten years, is the source of all. Now we ask that you look through our bodies and spirits, to return this boy from the edge of madness and his mother from the brink of long night."

Go-Shu took his place with the Seekers, grasping Si-Lun's shoulder, and the three braced themselves against the flood of force that coursed through them and the Shamal. As the light pulsed in the stone, the lad's eyes blinked, his head nodded forward, and he drooped into deep sleep.

"It is well with the small one," said the voice of Ru-Anh.

They moved now to the side of the woman, and Kla-Noh held the stone to her forehead. Again the current pulsed through them. They could see a faint flush begin to rise in the paper-whiteness of her taut cheek. The lines about her eyes smoothed away, and she sighed, with the first audible breath she had drawn since they entered the cave. There came a softening, a relaxation of her whole body, which warmed perceptibly beneath the hand of Kla-Noh.

The voice from the stone said again, "It is well."

Then the three loosed their grasp one upon the other, and slumped to sit upon the dusty floor of the cave.

After a time, Si-Lun drew a deep breath and rose to tend the fire, pulling the pot of broth into the edge of the coals as he completed the task. From the packs he brought their bowls and set them to warm. Then he filled one carefully, abstracted one of Kla-Noh's silver spoons from the packet, and sought to rouse the woman from her light sleep.

His gentle touch upon her shoulder at length drew her from lethargy, and she opened her great black eyes, seeming to stare up at him from a distance. He indicated the bowl and lifted her so that she might lie against his pack, half-sitting.

"This is good soup," he said quietly. "If you can swallow it, it will make you stronger."

The woman nodded and managed to sip from the spoon. The little effort exhausted her, yet she whispered as she sank back upon her pallet, "The child. My son . . . Le-Tho . . . where is he?"

"He sleeps against the wall," said Si-Lun, covering her again. "Soon he will waken, no longer in the grip of fear, and we shall give him broth and bread, and he will be well indeed."

Then she smiled and slept again.

Now Kla-Noh and Go-Shu found their feet and moved the child nearer the fire, pillowing his head upon a bed-

ding roll. Then he awoke, and for the first time, the spirit
of Le-Tho looked upon them from his eyes. He opened
his mouth obediently when a spoonful of broth was held
to his lips, and he smiled at the taste and reached for the
bread that Go-Shu offered him. When he was satisfied, he
lay quietly, watching the men move about the cave, making their own meal and readying the store of wood for
the coming night.

"There was fear," he whispered as Go-Shu paused beside him and touched his cheek. "All was black, and my
mother would not answer, and there was no food left. For
many days I was afraid, but when I was all alone in this
rock place with her and she never would open her eyes I
was very afraid."

"So would I have been," said Go-Shu, sitting on the
sand beside him. "Tell me, Le-Tho, where did you and
your mother come from, and how did you come here to
this place?"

"My father went to find a new place for us, for the island where we lived was very small and the family had
many houses there. He sent a boat for us, with men to
sail it, and my mother took our things and me and we
started to go to my father." The child's face grew
pinched.

"Those were bad men, for they would not go where my
mother told them. They took her jewels and all our
things, and they put us ashore where only rocks were.
They gave us a bag of food and our bedding rolls and
then they sailed away. So we walked up the hills where
there were trees, and my mother said that we must find
the houses of men, if we went far enough. But when we
came here, she said she could walk no more, so we came
in and she made torches and told me to light each just
before the last went out. And she lay down and was sick

for many days and would not eat. When I brought her water from the spring, she would drink, but I was afraid that she would die and leave me all alone."

Then tears flowed, but they were the gentle tears of relief, and they washed the last of the darkness from the youngling's spirit. And Go-Shu brought water and cloth and washed his face and took him upon his lap and talked and played with him as though he were the grandson of his heart.

The woman woke again and looked quietly on, smiling. Go-Shu set the child down beside her and knelt there.

"Alone I live, on a hill not many days' walk from this place. It would warm my heart should you come, with the child, to stay there until our friends may bring your man to fetch you. Loneliness is my chosen way of life, but the recent days have left me strangely lonely for human faces and voices, and the ways of the child delight me."

"It would be unwise to bring Le-Tho into a city of men," she said softly. "For he has yet to learn full control of his powers. So we will gladly be your guests until such time as my husband may come. For you seem a wise man, and a gentle one, and you have, with your companions, saved us both this day."

Then did Kla-Noh and Si-Lun agree that the plan was a wise one, and all lay down to rest.

In the night without the cavern the owls flitted and the wolves prowled and the small creatures hunted as was their wont. The lonely farmsteads were quiet beneath a new moon. And far to the south, Shar-Nuhn slept in peace beneath the stars.

XIII

The Star of San-Dah

The tender air of spring moved across the Purple Waters, caressing their waves into smoothly rolling patterns. From the south it blew, bringing the scent of greening meadows and young leaves. The terrace of Kla-Noh's house was awash with springtide, and the two Seekers sat idly, gazing across the bay toward Shar-Nuhn, which was turned into a fairy city by the evening light reflected from its garnet roofs and towers of amber-colored stone.

The east grew bluer, bluer yet, and the sun sank to the horizon. Night strode delicately up the sky, and the waters grew dark beneath. Then in the heart of the eastern heavens there blazed forth for the space of three heartbeats a point of light that glanced with pitiless brilliance and winked out, leaving its fiery afterimage across the sight of its beholders.

After a space in which the two watchers still gazed in astonishment toward the place where that starlike vision had been, Kla-Noh whispered, "That was like nothing I have ever seen. Many the trails of falling stars I have traced across the sky, many the comets I have tracked in lonely paths, but never have I seen a light in the sky such as that which we just have seen."

"Nor I," replied Si-Lun. "It seemed as if, for one instant, a window were opened between this world and one of bright wonder, before a hasty hand closed it again. Stars and planets I know as old friends who have guided me across the seas, but never did I meet that brilliant wanderer in any sky, until now."

Still they sat, looking to the east as if waiting for the light to reappear, but it did not. The sun drew after it the trailing bands of color from the west, and darkness mantled the whole of Shar-Nuhn. Then, as they sat, Si-Lun caught his breath sharply, as though a sudden pain had touched him.

"Are you ill?" asked Kla-Noh, rising and going to his side.

"Not ill," gasped Si-Lun through clenched teeth. "Something moves within me. Something is summoning. Take my hand, Kla-Noh, and join your thought to mine. Seek with me this thing that has gripped me."

Then the two clasped hands and were motionless in the darkness, striving through the runnels of their hearts, the mazes of their minds, to reach the secret thing that moved within the being of Si-Lun. It was like a pain, yet unlike, as Kla-Noh found when he took the young man's hand. It was a light within darkness, and a brilliance hidden in mist.

Then Kla-Noh gasped in comprehension. "The Shamal!" he said. "The Shamal calls us. Let us go inside, my son, and answer the gem, for there is the source of this sending which is within you."

At once they went to the cabinet where the topaz-colored crystal was kept, safe in a wrapping of silk and leather. The door of the cabinet was warm to the touch as the old Seeker turned the carven knobs and loosed the wrought catches. The leather was hot; and when he drew out the silken bindings, they almost burned his skin as he

removed them. The Shamal he laid quickly upon a table-
top, where it lay pulsing almost angrily against the cool
mosaic. No light was lit within the room, yet the fiery
glow of the crystal glanced from walls and ceiling as
though it were a little sun.

The Seekers knelt, one upon either side of the table,
gazing into the gem. "We are here. We are here. We are
here," they said, seeing their words sink into the stone as
pulsations of fire. "Who calls?" they asked; then, "And in
what can we aid you?"

Still the gem flickered, gathering strength from some
place beyond their knowledge. Yet they repeated their
words again and again, striving to reach across whatever
barrier was interposed, seeking to communicate with
whatever being sought them through the Shamal.

When it seemed as though the crystal must surely
burst into flame, there came a faint reply. "Li-Ah," it said.
"Li-Ah. There is need. There is need in the world of
Shanath, where dwell Li-Ah and her mother. Long have
we succored those in other worlds with words of wise advice. Now there is chaos, for the dread Star hangs at zenith and all is fallen into madness. Si-Lun she calls for,
and Kla-Noh, who aided her of old in another world than
ours. There is need of you in Shanath. Come to us. She
bade us tell you that the Initiates know the road. Go you
to them, and we shall await you. At sunset tomorrow in
your world, we shall be ready to receive you in ours.
Come to us, with the aid of the gods, come!"

The Shamal flickered. The light quivered upon its
faceted surface as cloud shadow across a lake. Slowly the
glow died, the warmth cooled. When the stone lay, once
more faintly luminous, upon the table between them,
Kla-Noh lifted it and wrapped it again.

Si-Lun moved to light the lamps. "Shall we call upon

the Initiates now?" he asked Kla-Noh, but the old Seeker shook his head.

"I am wiser now than I was," he said. "Now I husband my strength, that I may not use up the store before all my tasks are accomplished. The Initiates know when the Shamal is used. Only they, all believed, could use it or allow it to be used. Yet the voices in Shanath spoke through it, which surely means that the touch of Li-Ah, when last she walked in this world and made bright our house, attuned it also to her world. The Initiates, you may be sure, know what passed through the stone. They will be ready when we reach the Tower. To use the crystal now would weaken us, and we will need, I feel certain, all the vigor we possess."

They quieted their minds and went in to their evening meal, talking of other things and complimenting Nu-Veh upon his excellent cookery. After the meal was cleared away, they summoned Nu-Veh into the sitting room and told him of their impending absence.

"We shall take nothing with us, neither clothing nor food," said Kla-Noh. "You need prepare no packs. We ask only that you await our return with good patience and care for the house and the garden, that we may find all well when we return."

Then they retired, though it was not soon that sleep found their eyelids. In the drowsy spaces of their skulls they could see, each of them, a strange Star flowering in the eastern sky and the Shamal burning within their room, and they fell asleep at last to dream of Li-Ah and of a great Star bathing with chaotic brightness the unseen world of Shanath.

Morning found them busy about ordering their work and their studies for prolonged absence. Each looked upon his books and his instruments, his calculations and his carefully recorded diaries with a strange sadness.

"I find myself thinking, 'Shall I look upon these things, take up this pen, stroke this lute, pursue the delight of this calculation, ever again?'" said Si-Lun, drawing a cover over his work table.

"Truly," answered Kla-Noh, "the air sings with change. I look about me and all seems as a dream from which I have just awakened. Something within says, 'Look well, for you will not walk this way again,' wherefore I have made order of my affairs, that Nu-Veh and my kin may be cared for, should neither of us return from this strange journey."

When the sun reached its western arc, they were upon the Purple Waters, having made their good-byes and turned their backs upon the familiar. The Tower of Truth shone before them in mysterious splendor, its amber walls washed with the amethystine reflections of the sun-glanced sea, and their eyes sought to limn that transient glory upon their minds, as a reminder and an anchor when they walked upon another world.

The Father of Initiates stood at the door as they climbed the tall steps that led from the floor of the sea to the door of the Tower, then upward, pausing at each level of that great building yet flowing higher as if to reach the havens of the gods. And when they reached the great door, Ru-Anh took their hands, and there were tears upon his cheeks and in his beard.

"All is in readiness, my friends," he said. "We also heard the voices from Shanath, and we knew that you would come. There is peril in this journey; greatly do we fear it. The road through the chamber of the crystal will lead, this time, into an unknown place, and we will have little power over your safety."

"Yet must we go," said Kla-Noh. "You would not have us deny the call, Ru-Anh, and well do we know it."

"Then come and sup with us, in farewell and friendship," said the Initiate. "All of our number are gathered to do you honor, for you are as brothers of our order, though your ways have lain along different paths."

In truth, the whole complement of the Tower sat together in the eating chamber, and afterward each man and woman touched their hands and made the sign of blessing. Then they went up through the Tower to the chamber of the crystal and sat once again among the blue fires that shimmered within its walls, seeing the points of brightness flicker within the translucence, the room in the Tower grow dim and disappear.

When the quivering veil of blue dissolved, no robed figures of Initiates stood before them. The room into which they looked was curved into a hemisphere, and its walls glowed with rose-shot stone. Before a panel of palely shining instruments stood three tall women in gray-green draperies. As the last of the shimmer dissolved, they turned to the Seekers and hastened to help them rise.

"With hope have we awaited you," said the tallest. "We are Ri-La, Lu-Tha, and An-Re, servants of the Queen and of Li-Ah, her daughter. Much is there to tell you, but we must not, until you have eaten and rested. Yet know that you may bear in your hands the fate of all Shanath, for that which was long ago foreseen has come about, and all of the blood of Shanath walk in madness, without the walls of the Strongholds."

Though it had been evening in Shar-Nuhn, yet was it midday in the world to which they had come, and strange did it seem to lie down to sleep in full day. Yet their sleep was short and uneasy, and soon they rose and sought out Ri-La.

"Come with me," she said. "I must show you the city of Nir, which is the first city upon all the planet. Here the arts were born and the sciences flourish. Here is the tall house of the Queen, where Li-Ah now lies, struggling with madness."

Stricken dumb with apprehension, they followed, through halls that seemed built of rose quartz, past apartments, half-seen through open doors, that were filled with books and unrecognizable instruments. At last their guide paused before a portal that seemed molded of heavy metal, with enigmatic characters incised upon its face. Raising a silver whistle that hung from a chain about her neck, she trilled an odd melody, whereupon the door opened with a whisper of air but no other sound.

Utter darkness waited within. Almost tangible it was, seeming to brush against their faces with trailing webs as they followed Ri-La into the chamber. The door closed after them. The two Seekers stood capsuled in the isolation of the blind, waiting for their guide's proceeding. From the darkness there now grew a point of light, outlining the cup of her long hands as they held a gem, not unlike the Shamal, which waxed in brightness until it faintly illuminated the chamber. When the stone was well aglow, she moved to the wall and set it within a niche shaped nicely to fit just such a crystal.

With the seating of that gem, the whole wall of the chamber wakened into life. First it glowed green as a mountain stream shot with sunlight. Shifting patches of light and shadow moved within it that steadied, as the wall grew paler and brighter, until they formed into moving figures of men and women. They were seen from above, down a tremendous perspective of towers and thoroughfares. It seemed, for a time, that the figures were dancing. Then Kla-Noh exclaimed softly and laid his hand upon Si-Lun's shoulder. They peered intently into the wall, watching those milling forms. As though sensing their purpose, the wall drew nearer to the area, bringing the faces of the people into focus.

"They are all mad," breathed Kla-Noh, and Si-Lun nodded, never taking his eyes from the hysteric throng before them.

"This is Nir, and all places where the Star is now on high. So brilliant is its fire that it outshines the sun, and it will follow a track as the planet turns, round and round, and all whom its light touches will run mad. Where it was, there is exhausted slumber. Where it rises, there is awakening to new frenzy. While it is in the sky of Shanath, there are none to rule and none to serve, save only those of us whose lives are dedicated to the Strongholds. Their walls were made to hold out the rays of the Star of San-Dah, and dire were the warnings of those who builded them.

"Those of the royal blood sought to heed, but counselors scoffed and wheedled and after thousands of years the warnings dwindled into the mists of myth. Yet did the Fellowship of the Strongholds hold true to their beginnings and dwell within these places, making them the founts of wisdom for Shanath, and the sources of virtue. Now we, of all our fellows, are untouched by the Star, yet we cannot go out to aid even the Queen, for the touch of the Star would send us whirling with the rest, and leave none in all Shanath to seek help for our beleaguered world."

"And the Queen and Li-Ah—they are also thus?" asked Si-Lun, who had grown pale.

"I will show you," answered Ri-La, and she turned the

crystal in the niche. The wall whirled madly with dancing color, then settled into new patterns. Before them
was a bedchamber, cool with shadow. Upon the bed,
gripping its covering with both hands, lay Li-Ah, staring
straight upward as if she could see them. Shadows
danced across her smoke-blue eyes, which seemed held
open by force of will. They could see her lips move, and
Ri-La made an adjustment. Sound came from the wall.

"I will not. I will not. Madness is within me, yet I will
not let it overmaster me. Here will I lie until I wither to
dust, but I will not run through the streets as a hare before hounds." Her eyes closed, and her hands moved rest-
lessly upon the covers. They could see the effort that
held her tall form rigidly still upon the couch. Si Lun
cried out and stretched his hands toward her, as though
to reach and aid her.

"Nay," said Kla-Noh, touching his shoulder. "You cannot aid her thus. Now do I understand her need and the
purpose that strove even through madness to send word
to us. Wise is the lady, even when struggling with her
own spirit. For we alone upon this world may walk
abroad beneath the light of this terrible Star. And the key
to the problem lies in this."

"You believe that you can give help to Shanath?" asked
Ri-La. "There is a planet here, not only one city or one
land. Yet do I believe in the wisdom of Li-Ah. Mayhap
you will be able to succor our world."

"It may be that the answer lies within us," said Kla-
Noh. "Ri-La, should we move through the city to the
house where Li-Ah lies and bear her back within these
walls, would she then be free of madness?"

"Truly," answered the woman. "Had we but houses
made of Stronghold Stone, we might have saved the
world this travail. For the months that the Star hangs in

our sky, we could move at night about our necessary labors. We had thought to go ourselves after our ladies, but there were too many of the wild ones still moving about the streets, reeling with exhaustion, yet ready to rend us. We feared for our lives and we returned here."

"We be two who go where they will, madmen or no," said Si-Lun. "Make for us a map of the city of Nir, and mark upon it the swiftest and most secret way to the house of the Queen. We need not wait for nightfall, but may mingle with the whirling throngs and move through them as through the waves of the sea."

Then did Ri-La chart for them the path they must follow, and before nightfall they had made the fearful journey to the Queen's house. Strange was their task there, for they found that they must bind the two great ladies, whose bodies fought them while their eyes implored their aid. In strappings of silken sheets they wrapped them, and bore them back through the teeming thoroughfares where the people tore at them and at one another, reeling with weariness, yet unable to sink to rest so long as the light from the Star slanted from the horizon.

They entered the Stronghold, bearing within their arms the Queen of Shanath and her daughter, and they were greeted by the women with deep joy. For hours the ladies slept, and Kla-Noh and Si-Lun sought rest also, that they might be fresh when they met again with Li-Ah and her mother.

They awoke to the gentle voice of Lu-Tha, who whispered, "Our ladies wake, and would speak with you."

Strange was it to meet again with their old friend under skies other than those of Shar-Nuhn. But heartfelt was their greeting, and they turned to greet her mother. Then did they stand mute with wonder that any being could be so lovely. She was as Li-Ah would be when enriched with years and loving labors and deep thought. From her smoke-blue eyes shone wisdom wrapped in laughter, suffering conquered by strength. She was as all would be could they but find the way, and the Seekers knelt before her and took her hands.

"Lady, our lives are yours," they said. And she smiled at them and motioned for them to sit.

Then did Kla-Noh awaken from his amaze and become himself, practical and forthright. "Madam," he said, "there is a way to lighten this burden beneath which your realm is reeling. Answer me but two questions, and I will know whether it be in our power to work upon the entire planet."

"Surely I shall answer, Seeker. You have but to ask."

"Then these are they. Firstly, are there Strongholds scattered about all the populous places upon Shanath, as are the Towers of Truth in our world?"

"Aye, they are the sources of teaching and help and healing upon our world, much as the Towers are in yours. Few are the cities, and they sparsely tenanted, where there is not a Stronghold."

Kla-Noh spread his hands in satisfaction and his face told of his content. "Secondly," he said, "are there, in your medicines, powerful sleeping drugs, and large supplies of that which must be used in their compounding?"

"There are such medicines, but we must ask of Ri-La concerning their ingredients," answered the Queen.

Ri-La, being called, confirmed that there was no lack, in any part of the world, of the simple substances that formed such drugs.

"Then," said Kla-Noh, "obtain for us enough of these to send every inhabitant of Nir into deep slumber. Also cause to be made charts for Si-Lun and for me of every drinking well, no matter how hidden and obscure, in all the city. Should any of your number have the courage to venture out into the night, make charts for them also, and equip all with sleeping drugs. We shall put sleep in the wells, in the fountains, this night, that when the Star rises upon the morrow there may be no man or woman awake within the city. And as we do here, so may the Fellowship of the Strongholds do elsewhere, until all who may be reached sink into deep slumber."

"Surely this would make quiet the ways, yet what of the coming days?" asked the Queen.

"Not in one night, nor in one month, may the world be quieted," said Kla-Noh. "Yet each time many who are quiet with drug may be removed into the Strongholds. As they return to themselves, they also may go forth to save their fellows. Then all who are made normal may drug themselves into sleep at the rising of the Star, with measured doses designed to allow them to wake soon after Starset. Thus they may go about their business or aid the Fellowship with their labors in the hours of night. In days, there can be care and help for many or most. It can be done, Lady, if the Fellowship are strong in their dedication to the weal of their people."

"It shall be done," said the Queen, her eyes glowing with blue fires. "Ri-La, see you that all is set in motion. Compound the drugs and make the charts. We shall go out into the night and pour sanity into all the wells of Nir!"

Not in one night, nor in ten, was the task completed. Indeed, it was not completed at all, yet of all the people of Shanath who yet lived, few perished of hunger or illness or exhaustion after the project was set afoot. Those rescued from the madness gladly set themselves into the new pattern of drugged sleep by day and work by night, and they labored among their fellows with the zeal of the newly saved. And among them went the Queen and Li-Ah, never stinting of their efforts.

The Seekers did not count the days or the nights. As six men they strove, and all who worked by their sides marveled that two could contrive such accomplishment. But there came a day when they looked at the sky, before retiring to their couches, and saw that the Star was far and pale. Then they went to the top of the Stronghold, where was the Room of the Stars, and they asked of her who studied the heavens.

"In five more days the comet will be beyond the skies of Shanath," she said to them. "Five thousand years ago it came. In five thousand years it will come again. Pray to the gods that we do not allow the tale to become lost in myth, as happened before. The Stronghold Stone may save our far children from all, if we can but make the memory endure."

Then they went to the Queen and she heard them with joy. "If you had not come to our aid, then all save the Fellowship should long since have perished of starvation, of exposure, or the assaults of our fellows," she said. "Yet with your help we live, and are still a world of men. Surely there is no phrase in all of rhetoric sufficient to make our gratitude known to you."

"It is needless," said Kla-Noh. "When we were in need, over the long years, the voices of the Fellowship were in the wild, giving advice and comfort to all who learned the secret of communication. And when we called upon your daughter, she took a perilous road to come to us, in healing friendship. For me there is no need of any thanks. I am old, and if I may not be of service, why should I cheat the worms of their rightful prey?"

Then Si-Lun stepped forward and knelt at the Queen's knee. "No reward do I ask, no thanks, Lady, but a most audacious favor. Long have I looked upon your daughter with regard, keeping my thoughts to myself. Now do I ask leave to make them known to her, that she may examine her heart for a like affection for me. My presumption is terrible, yet this must I ask."

The Queen laid her hand lightly upon his gingery hair. "Think you, my son, that I have not seen your eyes when you looked upon her—or hers when she looked upon you? Only the dreadful exigencies that we have known have prevented your coming to understanding of your need for one another. Long has my daughter lived in the realms of thought and power, without seeking for companionship. Now has the time come when she must enter the world of humankind, taking up the solemn delights of that condition. Much do we need you in this battered world of Shanath. Long years of effort will it require to make good the damage, to repair and replace the lost, to reclaim and reteach those of the people whose madness does not wane with the waning star. Your strong hand will work with ours, your alien wisdom will supplement ours, your love will smooth the hard way in which Li-Ah must walk as she begins to share with me the arduous duties of rule. If it be your will."

The Queen stretched out her other hand to Li-Ah, who came to kneel beside Si-Lun. The mother looked deeply into the eyes of the daughter, then into those of the Seeker. She smiled. "If it be your will, join your hands together and you may rise from this spot as one, with the blessing of the gods and the goodwill of the Queen of Shanath."

Shyly, the two touched, and their hands locked together. They rose and stood before the Queen and Kla-Noh, dazzled by the thing that had happened to them so suddenly. Then Si-Lun turned from his bride and went to his old friend and father.

"For nothing less would I leave you alone, O Seeker," he said. "Yet here is my heart, here my work, for my life's length. And you are my benefactor. Had you not sought me out, one night long ago in the Dolphin Tavern, I should still be a joyless wanderer adrift upon our planet, without love, without usefulness. But your loneliness will be a bitter drop in my full cup."

Kla-Noh smiled upon the young man, and his was a smile of youthful joy. "Have no regret, taste no bitter drop, my son. I shall not return again to my house by the Purple Waters. Nu-Veh shall bring his family there, and his fat babies will roll where we sang and studied. For the Initiates have bidden me to the Tower, to be one with their company. Our good Ru-Anh, before our departure, besought me to join with them, should it be that we survived this venture and were able to return to Shar-Nuhn. And this I shall do, though a part of my heart shall remain here with you in Shanath."

The Queen laughed. "Be not so deadly solemn, my friends. Though we be of two worlds, yet there are many links between, and you need not be severed for all time by the sundering dimensions. And through your Shamal, Kla-Noh, may we ever speak with you and you with us, for we shall teach you the way. Be merry, children; be merry, Seeker. For though we now set forth into labor for many a long year, we stand upon a living world that might have been but a tomb, whirling about an uncaring universe. We live, we are united in love and understanding. There are many to aid, many to comfort, many to do battle with, did we but see the future. Yet for what else did the gods form us and set us within the cosmos?

Rejoice with me, before the gods, that we have lived to see the sun rise upon this day."

Then the Seekers' faces brightened, and their hearts grew light. They stood upon the world of Shanath, knowing that upon their own world, and this, and all the countless worlds within and without the cosmos, suns rose and set, by the will of the gods, and that men were a part of the purpose in the enigmatic mists of that which is. For an instant they saw their lives and their works as shining grains upon the strand of life, soon covered over but never lost, never futile.

Then they set hand in hand in a strong clasp and knew in their souls that space and time could never sunder the Seekers of Shar-Nuhn.